PRAISE FOR
CARLTON

"Easily the craziest, weirdest, strangest, funniest, most obscene writer in America."
—*GOTHIC MAGAZINE*

"Carlton Mellick III has the craziest book titles... and the kinkiest fans!"
—CHRISTOPHER MOORE, author of *The Stupidest Angel*

"If you haven't read Mellick you're not nearly perverse enough for the twenty first century."
—JACK KETCHUM, author of *The Girl Next Door*

"Carlton Mellick III is one of bizarro fiction's most talented practitioners, a virtuoso of the surreal, science fictional tale."
—CORY DOCTOROW, author of *Little Brother*

"Bizarre, twisted, and emotionally raw—Carlton Mellick's fiction is the literary equivalent of putting your brain in a blender."
—BRIAN KEENE, author of *The Rising*

"Carlton Mellick III exemplifies the intelligence and wit that lurks between its lurid covers. In a genre where crude titles are an art in themselves, Mellick is a true artist."
—*THE GUARDIAN*

"Just as Pop had Andy Warhol and Dada Tristan Tzara, the bizarro movement has its very own P. T. Barnum-type practitioner. He's the mutton-chopped author of such books as *Electric Jesus Corpse* and *The Menstruating Mall*, the illustrator, editor, and instructor of all things bizarro, and his name is Carlton Mellick III."
—*DETAILS MAGAZINE*

Also by
Carlton Mellick III

Satan Burger
Electric Jesus Corpse (Fan Club Exclusive)
Sunset With a Beard (stories)
Razor Wire Pubic Hair
Teeth and Tongue Landscape
The Steel Breakfast Era
The Baby Jesus Butt Plug
Fishy-fleshed
The Menstruating Mall
Ocean of Lard (with Kevin L. Donihe)
Punk Land
Sex and Death in Television Town
Sea of the Patchwork Cats
The Haunted Vagina
Cancer-cute (Fan Club Exclusive)
War Slut
Sausagey Santa
Ugly Heaven
Adolf in Wonderland
Ultra Fuckers
Cybernetrix
The Egg Man
Apeshit
The Faggiest Vampire
The Cannibals of Candyland
Warrior Wolf Women of the Wasteland
The Kobold Wizard's Dildo of Enlightenment +2
Zombies and Shit

Crab Town
The Morbidly Obese Ninja
Barbarian Beast Bitches of the Badlands
Fantastic Orgy (stories)
I Knocked Up Satan's Daughter
Armadillo Fists
The Handsome Squirm
Tumor Fruit
Kill Ball
Cuddly Holocaust
Hammer Wives (stories)
Village of the Mermaids
Quicksand House
Clusterfuck
Hungry Bug
Tick People
Sweet Story
As She Stabbed Me Gently in the Face
ClownFellas: Tales of the Bozo Family
Bio Melt
**Every Time We Meet at the Dairy Queen,
Your Whole Fucking Face Explodes**
The Terrible Thing That Happens
Exercise Bike
Spider Bunny
The Big Meat
Parasite Milk
Stacking Doll
Neverday
The Boy with the Chainsaw Heart
Mouse Trap

SNUGGLE
CLUB

CARLTON MELLICK III

ERASERHEAD PRESS
PORTLAND, OREGON

ERASERHEAD PRESS
P.O. BOX 10065
PORTLAND, OR 97296

WWW.ERASERHEADPRESS.COM

ISBN: 978-1-62105-311-8

AUTHOR'S NOTE

So I haven't been writing a whole lot lately. You might have noticed that my book releases have not been as frequent in the past year and a half. I apologize for this, especially for those of you who look forward to three or four book releases from me every year. But I needed some time off. My father, Carlton Mellick II, died recently (and without warning) of a pulmonary embolism, so I've been dealing with grief and helping my mother get her life in order. If you've ever lost a parent you probably understand what I've been going through. It's been pretty traumatic and has had an impact on me both physically and psychologically. But I think I'm now ready to move on. It's a new year, my mom's doing fine, the world isn't ending, and I feel like I can finally get back to all the projects I was excited about before my life was thrown off course.

The only problem is that it's not easy getting back into writing after taking such a long hiatus. It also isn't easy getting back into writing after the death of someone close to you. So I decided to write a couple practice books to warm me back up. These books were just meant to get me over my emotional slump and get me back into a working state of mind. They weren't even supposed to ever be published.

Snuggle Club is the first of the two practice books (the other is called *The Bad Box*). It was never actually meant to be read by anyone. I wrote it for myself. You could say it was my way of writing my way out of grief while at the same time doing something easy and fun and distracting. It very nearly ended up being deleted the second I finished it but there was a part of me that was really happy with it. There's nothing groundbreaking or earth-shattering about it, no aspects that top any book I've previously written, but it's a fun little diversion that I feel is worth a read until my next project.

So here it is. My 60th book. I hope you enjoy it.

Wait a minute… This is my 60th book? I've written 60 books now? How the hell did that happen?

—Carlton Mellick III 1/14/2020, 8:14pm

First Rule of
Snuggle Club

**Everyone gets snuggled at
Snuggle Club.**

CHAPTER
ONE

I never knew losing a loved one would be so exhilarating.

When the most important person in your life dies, you'd expect it would take all the life out of you, suck every ounce of energy from your flesh and leave you just a sniveling, weeping husk on the ground. I assumed I'd spend months or years lying in bed, so depressed I couldn't move or eat or accomplish anything but stagger to the kitchen every time I needed a fresh bottle of vodka or a new pot to puke in. But this isn't what happened to me. Ever since Julie died, I've never felt more invigorated in all my life. I'm so full of energy that I can't sit still. I need to keep moving, keep doing things, at all times of the day.

I've cleaned my house from top to bottom forty-seven times this month. I've organized my vintage toy collection twenty-three times. I've coordinated the clothes in my closet from formal to business casual to couch slob. I've painted my garage pink and orange. I've done my taxes and back taxes. I've cooked twenty-eight bell pepper casseroles. I've built shelves in the basement and painted thirty-six still life paintings even though I haven't touched a paintbrush since high school.

But the most surprising thing is how much exercise I've been doing. I typically loathe exercising, especially exercising in public. I've always found it embarrassing for some reason—letting other people see me sweat and pant and make ugly faces as I catch my breath after only ten minutes of physical activity. It took my wife's death to stop me from caring about what other people thought of me. Embarrassment doesn't seem to matter as much now that the worst possible thing has already happened.

I run at least ten miles a day. Usually four miles in the morning, three in the afternoon and three late at night when everyone else in the neighborhood is asleep. I do a hundred pushups, a hundred sit-ups, and a hundred squats on the hour every hour that I'm not running, pushing myself so hard that I'm probably doing more damage to my body than good. But I can't help myself. No matter how much work I do or how much exercise I get, I never seem to tire. I just can't sit still.

I'm pretty sure I'm still in shock. It's the adrenalin coursing through my body that won't let me rest. This is supposed to be normal. Everyone experiences this. But I thought it would have ended after a few days. It's been three months and there's no sign of it letting up.

I've never thought of having a life without Julie. We spent every waking moment together. We worked the same job. We had the same interests. We didn't have any plans for our future that didn't involve each other. The idea that she's no longer here with me doesn't make sense. It can't possibly be real. I have to keep running, keep cleaning, keep busy until she comes back home to me.

Although I've been insanely productive with a variety of tasks over the past few months, there are certain activities I've found impossible to do at all. Reading, playing video games, watching movies—these are all the things Julie and I loved doing together, but are impossible for me to do now, alone. I also haven't been eating much of anything. Nothing has flavor. I keep cooking casseroles and pies and cookies, but I don't eat any of them. I just put them in Tupperware and freeze them until I run out of room in the icebox outside.

But the thing that I've had the hardest time with is sleeping. I haven't slept alone in over fifteen years. I don't even know how to sleep without my wife pressed up against me. The comfort of her warmth against mine is what put me to sleep every night. I was much smaller than her, both shorter and thinner, so she was the big spoon and I was the small. Her arms and legs wrapped around me so comfortably that it felt like every inch of her body was embracing mine, like she had the ability to morph into a blanket of flesh that oozed over me, purring and pulsing and melting me into a puddle of coziness that instantly sunk me into a deep sleep.

Snuggling was our favorite thing to do together. Better than eating or movie-watching or playing video games or even having sex. If we had the opportunity to quit our jobs and just snuggle together fulltime forever we would do that and never get bored. We always imagined the day that we could retire as little old people who snuggled away our twilight years together. But now that Julie's dead, the snuggles died with her. I'll never marry anyone else. I'll never snuggle anyone ever again.

I've tried sleeping with heavy blankets wrapped around me, pretending they were her. I've tried buying large stuffed animals and filling them with hot water bottles. I've even thought about buying one of those realistic latex sex dolls and dressing it up as Julie, but they don't make them in the same body shape as hers and even if they did I'm sure it wouldn't be good enough to trick me into thinking that it was the real thing no matter how much it was designed to look like her. I just need Julie back. I need her to return to life and crawl into our bed and snuggle with me. If this doesn't happen I'll never be able to sleep again.

When I first heard about cuddle parties, they sounded like the creepiest, weirdest social gathering anyone could ever partake in. A group of strangers get together in their pajamas and snuggle each other like human-shaped teddy bears? Who in the world would be interested in such a thing? You'd have to be the loneliest, most pathetic kind of person to have any desire to partake in such an activity. I've never been to an orgy, but even orgies make more sense than cuddle parties. I'd be much less embarrassed to tell people I was going to an orgy than I would to a group cuddle session.

But now, lying awake in my cold lonely bed, cuddle parties are starting to make complete sense to me. I don't want to get into another relationship. I don't want to find somebody to replace Julie. But I do need somebody to snuggle with. I need to feel another person's body against mine. Perhaps, if I find the right person, it might even remind me of being with Julie again. Perhaps I can even pretend, just for a moment, that it was her body pressed against mine instead of some stranger's.

Searching online, I discovered the cuddle community was much larger than I expected. There was a different snuggle gathering scheduled almost every day of the week in almost every neighborhood in town. Some were exclusive, private gatherings that took place in the hosts' living rooms. Others were open to the public and encouraged newcomers. But there was one that actually had a storefront and was open five days a week—a business named Cuddle Me! that had seventeen locations across the country. I decided that would be the one to try. I didn't like the idea of showing up at some strange person's house demanding to be snuggled. A more public setting would make it easier to escape if things got too uncomfortable. It also would probably be more inviting to people on the quiet, socially awkward side like myself.

I'm not expecting much from attending a cuddle party. I really don't think it's going to fill the hole in my heart or even help me sleep better at night. But if there's any chance at all that I can feel the same warmth as I did when I snuggled with Julie then it is worth a shot.

The Cuddle Me! storefront is in the worst possible place that it could be: in the strip mall right next to my work. I hoped it would be on the other side of town, somewhere that I normally don't frequent just in case anyone recognizes me. But it's right there between the Panera Bread and the California Pizza Kitchen, two places that many of my coworkers visit during lunch break or meet at after work.

I'd hate to run into anyone I know as I walk into the weird cuddling place. Not just because it would be awkward explaining myself but because I know I've been taking way too much bereavement time and don't want to have to go back to work. If I get caught I'm sure the news would get to David and he'd assume I'm well enough to return. That's a conversation I don't want to have.

I'm parked out front of Cuddle Me!, the engine still running, wondering whether or not I should leave and come back during the late-night session. There are people going in and out of California Pizza Kitchen. Nobody I recognize, but quite a few people. All of them are passing by the Cuddle Me! entrance, pointing and laughing or just looking confused when they read the sign.

The sign reads: Everyone gets cuddled at Cuddle Me!

I don't see anyone actually entering the cuddle shop. Perhaps the website was wrong about the hours of the afternoon session. Or perhaps it's so unpopular that nobody is showing up. I have no idea how such a place can even stay in business in such a high traffic location unless they have a dedicated clientele. Squinting my eyes, I don't see anything inside. The windows are blacked out, probably to keep it private from inquisitive eyes. It seems empty. Closed. There are no signs that indicate whether the place is open or not, but until I see someone going inside, I'm just going to have to assume the cuddle party isn't happening at this time.

Just as I shift into reverse and begin pulling out of the parking space, there's a knock on the driver's side window. The vibrations on the glass are so loud and unexpected that I scream like a teenage girl in a horror movie and slam on the brakes. A woman bends down, peeking through the window at me. At first, I think that it's Susan from Accounting. They both have the same bright red hair, frizzy and poorly dyed. The same wrinkles in the eyes that make them look like they spent way too much time sunbathing in their youth. The same blue and green and red makeup that makes me wonder if they're going for a Fourth of July fireworks kind of look.

But it's not Susan from accounting. It's some other person. She just stares at me, waiting for me to roll down the window. I put the car in park and turn off the engine so I can hear what she has to say. But I don't roll the window down. She looks like she could be some kind of crazy person.

When our eyes meet, she asks, "Are you here to snuggle?"

A smile stretches across her crusty lips.

I don't know what to say other than, "Ummm…"

"Of course you are!" she says, "I saw you eyeballing the entrance!"

She grabs the handle and pulls on it three times, trying to get the door open. Even though the door is locked, her actions make me jump so high that I rip the keys from the ignition and drop them on the floor.

"It's okay to be nervous," she says, still pulling on the door handle. "Everyone's nervous their first time."

I reach for the keys under my seat, my hands shaking so frantically that I can't get a grip on them. I feel like I'm in a low budget horror movie where I'm fumbling with my keys as a monster tries to break in before I can get away.

Once I get a good grip on the keychain, I hear a loud click as the doors unlock. My elbow must have pushed the button on the armrest. When the woman opens the door, I realize there's no escape. I can't just drive away without talking to her.

"My name's Cherry," she says, leaning her head inside the car between me and the steering wheel, holding out her hand to shake.

I don't have any choice but to shake it, putting the keys in my jacket pocket and gripping her hand.

"I'm Ray."

Her hand is unusually cold to my touch. Her fingers thin and bony, the skin so loose that it could probably be pulled two inches off the back of her hand without much effort.

"Nice to meet you, Ray," says the woman. "I'm the cuddle party facilitator. It's my job to make sure you feel safe and comfortable."

If she's in charge of the cuddle party, she must be terrible at her job. I haven't even stepped inside and I already don't feel safe or comfortable. I'm beginning to think I made a terrible mistake.

"If you don't think you're ready to go in, you can wait out here with me. I don't mind." She leans in closer, almost like she's planning to lay her head on my lap. "It's sometimes easier to participate when you enter with a friend."

I shake my head, noticing all the Panera Bread customers staring at us. "No, I'm fine. We can go in."

She closes her eyes and nods her head slowly. "I understand you. You have good vibes."

She lingers with half her body inside my car before she gives me enough breathing room to get out.

"A lot of people think cuddle parties are weird and awkward," Cherry says. "But they're not awkward at all. You'll see. Everyone's really respectful and down to earth. You'd think a social gathering like this would attract a lot of weirdos, but nobody's creepy at all."

I grab my backpack from the backseat, lock the doors and step onto the sidewalk, making sure nobody sees me approach the entrance. Before I can sneak inside, Cherry blocks my way. She lingers, still wanting to talk.

"I've been going to cuddle parties for over five years now and they've really changed my life. Did you know that physical contact is necessary for positive mental wellbeing? Even more so than exercising and maintaining a healthy diet. Humans need regular physical contact in order to be happy."

I try to get around Cherry before somebody I know shows up. "I've never heard of that."

"It's all scientifically proven," she says, nodding. "That's why Cuddle Me! is such an important business. Cuddle parties are just as essential as gyms and restaurants. Everyone needs a place they can go to cuddle no matter what their relationship status might be. I haven't been in a serious relationship in years but my physical needs are still completely satisfied."

I'm having a hard time staying in one spot. Before I can hold back, I find myself blurting out, "It sounds kind of like an orgy if you ask me… Only weirder."

Cherry laughs and shakes her head. "Oh, no, not at all. You don't have to worry about that. It's completely different from an orgy." She pauses for an awkward amount of time and then says, "But, now that you mention it…" She leans in, lowering her voice. "I organize those as well. If you're interested just let me know and I'll fill you in on the next meetup."

I nearly choke on my own spit when she says this.

"No," I tell her firmly. "Thank you, but no. I don't have any interest in that at all."

She backs off. "Of course, of course. The offer still stands, though. No pressure."

I wonder what Julie would say if she saw me right now, talking to this woman about orgies and cuddle parties. She'd probably laugh her ass off at me. She always thought it was funny whenever I got myself into embarrassing situations like this one.

Second Rule of Snuggle Club:

It costs only $139.99 for a membership to Snuggle Club. Be sure to pre-pay online before attending each session.

CHAPTER
TWO

The inside of the cuddle shop looks a bit like a yoga studio, full of floor mats and mirrors. It probably was a yoga studio at one point. But there's also an arrangement of big fluffy pillows, beanbag chairs, and stuffed animals scattered across the floor. There are seven people inside already, all wearing bright-colored pajamas with hearts or little animals on them, sitting on beanbag chairs in a circle, chatting with each other. They all seem to be old friends.

Once we're inside, Cherry closes the door and locks it behind her with a key that only she possesses. I instantly feel trapped, unable to escape unless I ask permission.

When she sees the uneasy look on my face, Cherry says, "It's so that you'll feel more comfortable. We don't want anyone barging in on us during the snuggle session, do we?"

Despite her response, I'm convinced it's because she's more worried about people escaping than entering.

"Go put on your pajamas in the back," she tells me, pointing to a door on the far side of the room.

When she says this, all the other people in the room stop talking and look in my direction. They glare at me like I'm intruding on their private space, like I don't belong in their snuggle clique. I'm fine with it, though. I almost hope that they tell me I'm not welcome and ask me to leave. It would give me an easy way out.

But they don't say anything. They just stare as I walk slowly through their circle and go for the door in the back. The second I step into the changing room, their voices burst into laughter, going back to chatting and giggling as they had when I entered.

The changing room is very similar to the dressing room of a department store, only it's mixed-gender. There are four changing booths lining the walls. Only one of them is still occupied.

As I take an empty stall, I hear crying from the one at the end. A young woman's cries. As I open my backpack and pull out my pajamas, the girl's sobs grow louder. I lean down and look under the divider. She's two stalls down, sitting on the bench, her pants dropped down to her ankles as though she burst into tears in the middle of changing her clothes.

I wonder if I should ask her what's wrong, if there's anything I can do for her. But then I decide that would probably make her more uncomfortable. As I get dressed, I wonder what could possibly be wrong. Did one of the men harass her just before I arrived? Or is she here for the same reason I am? Perhaps she lost her significant other and came to the cuddle party with a desperate need to connect with another person. Either way, I feel really bad for the girl. But I have to just ignore her. If I was the person hiding in a changing stall, crying my heart out, the last thing I'd want is some strange person asking me what's wrong. I decide to just leave her be and go out to join the others.

I'm seated next to a large man with a thick beard and tiny glasses. He doesn't look like the kind of guy who would participate in a cuddle party. He looks more like the kind of guy who would ride a Harley and kick your ass at a roadhouse bar for looking at him funny.

Cherry squishes a beanbag chair exactly twelve times before she sits on it, as though it needed to be just the perfect shape to accommodate her comfort demands.

When seated, crossing her legs in a yoga position, she lets out a long sigh and says, "So how's it snuggling, everyone?"

They all smile and nod their heads, saying, "It's snuggling great!"

I divert my eyes, completely embarrassed by interacting with these people. I had no idea they'd have their own snuggle lingo.

"I've been snuggling just fine myself," Cherry says.

"I've been looking forward to this session all day."

Then Cherry gets into the rules of the cuddle party. She talks about how your pajamas must stay on at all times, how nobody has to snuggle with anyone they don't want to, how no means no and yes means yes, and what kind of touches are appropriate and inappropriate. Just the fact that she has to spell out all of the inappropriate ways to touch each other while cuddling makes me even more uncomfortable than if she didn't say them at all, because it proves that there were enough creepy people attending this in the past that they had to put these rules into place. Like if she didn't clearly explain this in precise detail it is exactly what would have happened. What's worse is that she has the large bearded guy come up and demonstrate exactly what would be inappropriate by grabbing his balls through his pajamas and having him grab her boobs and squeeze them.

"This is a cuddle party no-no," Cherry says, as her hand lingers in the man's crotch. "I don't want to see any of this."

When the bearded man sits back down, everyone introduces themselves. Going around the room, starting from Cherry's right, an older woman of about sixty-five introduces herself.

"Hello, my name is Helen and I'm a cuddle addict," she says and giggles. Everyone else giggles with her.

Was that supposed to be some kind of lame Alcoholics Anonymous joke or do we really have to introduce ourselves that way?

Helen waves her hands to calm everyone down. "I

kid." She looks directly at me. "We kid here."

Somebody please shoot me now.

Helen puts her hand on her chest and continues, "This is my tenth cuddle session and it's just been a blast coming to these with all of you. Ever since Roger was put on chemotherapy I haven't been able to get any good cuddles in." She looks at me again, as though I'm the only one who doesn't understand. "You can't cuddle anyone when they're on chemotherapy. Their sweat is radioactive. He's been sleeping in the guest room while I have the big lonely bed all to myself."

The woman next to her takes her hand and puts it in her lap, then lays her head on her shoulder to comfort her.

"Roger doesn't know I've been coming here," she continues. "I don't want to cause him any extra stress. But physical contact is really important to me. I don't function properly without snuggling at least once a day. I'm sure Roger will understand once I explain it to him, once he's feeling better."

The next person to introduce herself is the youngest in the group, but she appears to be even older than Helen. She dresses like an old lady, wears her hair like an old lady, has the sagging facial features of somebody at least seventy years old. She even has an old lady name: Edna.

When Edna introduces herself, she says, "I'm twenty-two years old and haven't had a boyfriend in my whole life." The tone of her voice is slow and sad. The expression on her face is even sadder. "I wasn't allowed to date when I was in high school. I was too busy studying in college to even attend a single party, let alone have time for a guy.

Not that anyone would have dated me anyway. Nobody has ever found me the least bit attractive."

I'm getting depressed just listening to her. She must be the least confident person I've ever met and probably spends the majority of her time feeling sorry for herself. I'm not sure if I should pity her or do something to help boost her self esteem.

"I know this isn't a place to find a boyfriend," she continues, "and I know I'm on probation for trying to contact guys I liked after a few sessions, but it's the only place I can go where I can feel what it's like to be in a relationship." Her eyes light up and she smiles slightly. It's the first time she's been able to indicate that she's capable of expressing even an ounce of happiness. "I like to think of each cuddle as a five-minute love affair, as if the person I'm embracing is my long-term boyfriend, maybe even my husband or my fiancé." The smile grows wider on her face. It's almost scary and unnatural, as though the muscles around her mouth are so used to frowning that they don't understand what to do with a smile. "Sometimes I like to imagine that we've just finished a long passionate lovemaking session and are now holding each other in the blissful aftermath. Or maybe we are snuggling on our wedding night in the big mansion we just moved into, envisioning our beautiful future together. Or maybe I imagine we are lovers who vowed to commit suicide together to escape a world that does not understand or respect us, drinking poison or taking pills and holding each other as our lives slowly slip away." She pauses for a moment, her eyes drifting off into space, as though imagining how romantic that kind of death would be. Once she snaps out of it, she says, "Either way, I like to fantasize a lot when I'm snuggling. I have whole backstories for everyone. It's really fun that way."

I knew there'd be a lot of creeps who would go to cuddle parties, but I just assumed they'd all be guys trying to hook up. It turns out that women are just as capable of being creeps as men. After Edna finishes and I look around the room, nobody else seems at all disturbed by her words. It's like everything she said is perfectly normal for a cuddle party. But, then again, am I any worse? I'm coming to this thing hoping that I can pretend the person I snuggle with is my dead wife. I'm sure most of the girls in this room would be creeped out if they learned that about me. The only thing that differentiates me from Edna is that there's no fucking way I'd ever admit my fantasies to the group.

The next person to be introduced is an overly tanned white guy wearing hemp pajamas unbuttoned halfway down his chest, spikes gelled into his bleached blond hair, and for some reason wearing a pair of Oakleys circa 1995 on his forehead. He calls himself DJ Tanner. I'm not sure if that's his DJ name or if DJ is his first name and Tanner his last. Either way, he definitely seems like a DJ.

"I'm into experiences, you dig?" DJ Tanner says. "Experiences that get me high. Ever since rehab I've been clean, I don't touch any drugs at all not even weed or alcohol, but I still need to get high on something, you know what I'm saying?" DJ Tanner doesn't seem capable of speaking without moving his hands. Every word out of his mouth causes his arms to wave around in circles. He nearly slaps Edna in the face as he continues, "Sure I like the rush of rock-climbing and skydiving and snowboarding, but snuggling is a different kind of high. When you touch your body against another person's, there's an explosion of endorphins, especially when it's with somebody you don't know or with a whole group of people. I'm cool snuggling guys, too. I go both ways." He lowers his Oakleys and leans further back into his chair." Most of you all know me. You know I'm down with the snuggles. Nobody regrets snuggling with me. I'm a fucking snuggle champion, you dig?"

I'm not sure if that was a back story or a sales pitch, but either way I'm happy when DJ Tanner stops talking. He's perhaps the most annoying person in the group so far and I pity anyone who has to deal with him on a regular basis.

The next two guys to speak are just as bad as DJ Tanner. Maybe even worse. They both look to be mid-thirties lonely guys who think a cuddle party would be a good place to hook up. Both of them used the line that they wanted to try cuddle parties to "get more in touch with their sensitive sides" while staring at the women's cleavage.

While they speak, I zone out, not interested in hearing a single word they're saying. Instead, I focus on a woman entering from behind us, the same woman I heard crying in the changing room. She seems to be in her late thirties, the same age as I am. Long messy dirty blonde hair, black pajamas with thin gray stripes, her eyes puffy from crying so much. She sits down in a beanbag chair several feet away from the rest of the group, not making eye contact with anyone, staring at the ground and holding her breath, as though fighting the urge to cry again.

When the guy in front of her finishes talking, Cherry decides to pick on the girl hiding in the back even though it clearly isn't her turn to speak next.

Cherry says, "Melody, why don't you go? It's been a while since your last cuddle party. I'm glad to see you return."

The woman raises her head with an alarmed look, almost surprised that anyone noticed her back there.

"Ummm…" she says, wiping tears from her eyes to make herself presentable. "Okay… sure."

Melody clears her throat and sits up straight. Then she squeezes her knees together and folds her hands into her lap.

After she introduces herself, she says, "I've been coming to cuddle parties for three years now, off and on." Long pauses between every sentence. "Those who know me are probably already aware of my condition. Ever since, you know, the attack… I've not felt comfortable with other people touching me, especially members of the opposite sex. I come to cuddle parties in order to get over this fear, to be able to touch somebody without it causing a panic attack. My therapist thinks these are very healthy for me. She says that they are good stepping stones in a safe setting…" She notices all of the eyes on her and looks down at the floor. "I still freak out whenever somebody brushes against me at the grocery store or stands too close to me in a crowded elevator, but I'm now able to shake a man's hand without having a panic attack. I'm able to hold a conversation with my boss. I don't assume that all men are dangerous."

As she says this, all the women in the room lean in and nod their heads, trying to console Melody with their eyes. All the men, on the other hand, shrink in their chairs and avoid eye contact, almost feeling guilty by association. I think the whole thing is tragic but have no idea how it would feel to be her. I've known both women and men who have gone through such trauma, and from what I understand, it can completely, utterly destroy people, even worse than one might expect. I really wouldn't want to cuddle with somebody with that much apprehension, but I'm glad the cuddle parties have helped her heal. At least they are good for something.

The burly bearded man introduces himself as Dan. His voice is a complete contradiction to his stature. He speaks in a very soft, delicate tone. He's not a big ass-kicking biker like I first assumed. He's more like a big hairy hippy.

"I'm the assistant facilitator who helps Cherry with

these meetings. You'll see a lot of me if you're a regular to these sessions." He rubs his chin and leans forward, as though trying to think of something profound to say. "I see cuddling as something holistic and meaningful. When we come together physically, it's an exploration of each other's souls. Our auras weave into one and…"

With that, I completely block him out. I'm not interested in listening to his hippy new age garbage. It's cool that he's into it but I couldn't care less about anything he has to say on the matter. I love snuggling as much as anybody but that doesn't mean I'm going to buy that it's some kind of spiritual journey two people explore together. I'm just trying to heal, like Melody. I couldn't give a shit about cuddle parties otherwise.

So while Dan continues his speech, I think more about what I'm going to say to the group. I have to introduce myself next and am not quite sure how much information to give the group. I don't want to be viewed as a pity case, but I also don't want anyone thinking I'm like the other pervy guys who are obviously just here to creep on women.

But before I can figure out what I'm going to say to the group, Dan finishes speaking and Cherry calls on me. All eyes look in my direction. As the newest member of the group, it seems everyone's pretty interested in hearing what I'm all about.

Without any ideas of how to lie, I decide to tell them the truth:

"My name's Ray. I've never been to a cuddle party before. To be completely honest, I always thought they were pretty weird. I mean, what kind of weirdo goes to a group for cuddling?" I let out a nervous laugh, but nobody laughs with me. Most of them look a little annoyed. I clear my throat and reposition myself in the beanbag chair. "So… my wife died a few months ago. Car accident." I feel everyone's eyes relax on me, not quite as annoyed as they were a second ago. "Not exactly a car accident, though. Her car was parked on the side of the road and she was checking her phone for messages. She always refused to text when she drove, even before it became a law. Don't want to cause an accident, right?"

I smile and let out some kind of cross between a laugh and a cry. I realize in this moment that I haven't spoken to anyone about Julie's death before now. Not friends, not family, not even a therapist.

Hesitating only for a moment, I decide it's fine to let it out. Who cares what these people think, anyway?

"She was in the middle of texting me when the car hit her. I was arguing with her about what we should have for dinner. She always picked up dinner for us because I hated going into restaurants, even for takeout. She was fine with going out alone, but she never knew what to get. We used to have the stupidest arguments, just over dinner. She never cared what we'd eat. Anything was fine with her. But I'm different. Food is important to me. Only I can't get excited about what I'm eating unless the person I'm sharing a meal with is just as excited about it as I am. So we'd have these ridiculous back-and-forths about what to have. I wanted to know what food would make her happy, but she didn't care. Thai food?

Mexican? Jersey Mike's? How about sushi? You love sushi. And she'd just say, 'whatever you want.' And for some reason that would piss me off. Why didn't she ever have a preference? Why couldn't she get excited about eating something, just once? We used to go for hours like this. Just trying to figure out what to eat. It was so stupid. And it would almost always turn into a huge argument because we'd be starving and cranky and just want the other person to make a decision. Usually, we'd just end up getting drive-thru burritos at the 24-hour taqueria because all other options were closed by then. That's how Julie died—in a texting argument about what stupid burrito I wanted from the stupid 24-hour burrito shop we ate at five days a week. I remember being so pissed off at her for taking so long. My last text said I wanted a simple California burrito with guacamole and a large horchata. No response. No 'okay, I'll get that and be home soon.' The drunk driver plowed into the driver's side door and she was dead before I even clicked send. Two hours passed and no word from her. Nothing. I was starving and cranky and pissed off from our argument. I thought maybe she was annoyed with me and went to a friend's house or went out for drinks. I even thought maybe, being a paranoid idiot, she was screwing some other guy because she was sick of my bullshit. But she was dead. I got the call from the hospital. They said she passed away. I had no fucking clue what they were talking about. How the hell was she dead? Who the hell would call me and tell me this? It had to be a mistake. They had to have the wrong number. They had to be talking about somebody else… But when I saw the body, I knew it was true. She was dead. She died because I couldn't decide what stupid fucking burrito to eat five minutes sooner…"

When I stop and look up, I notice everyone is looking at me with very quiet faces. I realize I might have just out-crazied all of the crazy people in the room.

But then somebody breaks the quiet. The girl next to me, the only one who hasn't spoken yet, says, "You're like me."

I turn to her. She's a younger woman with short brown hair and a dark complexion. Her eyes are large and soft, leaning forward to me as though she wants to give me a hug.

"You came here for physical comfort after losing your loved one," she says.

I nod.

"That's why I'm here as well," she says.

I'm no longer able to speak, so I let her take over. She introduces herself as Amaya and tells her story of how her boyfriend committed suicide last year. He had difficulty with depression ever since he was a child, but it never was much of a problem. His episodes went as quickly as they came. So it was a shock when she came home one day and found him hanging from the bathroom door. She couldn't believe it. She thought they were happy together. She thought they'd be together forever.

Like me, she decided to come to the cuddle party in order to heal. She wanted to feel a man's embrace without being in a relationship. She even admitted that she likes to pretend to cuddle with her dead boyfriend whenever she's with another man at the cuddle party.

I'm sure she's the reason I'm here. She's the person I need. The other women at the cuddle party freak me out a little too much. I really don't want to get anywhere near them. But Amaya understands. She's the perfect person to help me with Julie's death.

But when the group breaks and the cuddle session is about to begin, I realize that all the other guys have the same idea. They all want to cuddle with Amaya. It makes sense. She's young, pretty, nice, and down to earth. She doesn't have the same issues as the other women at the cuddle party. I have no idea what I'm going to do now.

Third Rule of Snuggle Club:

Pajamas stay on at all times. Bikinis, tank tops, boxer briefs, latex cat suits, and cut-off jean shorts are no longer acceptable attire at Snuggle Club.

CHAPTER
THREE

Even though I was sitting right next to Amaya, it's one of the douchey guys from across the room that gets to her first. He nearly lunges across the yoga mats at her, waving his hands and crying out to let him cuddle her. She agrees with a smile and a nod. Then they find a place in the corner full of pillows and stuffed animals and go immediately into spooning.

Dan partners up with Helen and Cherry with one of the other douchey guys. But everyone else in the room just stares at each other, sitting in their beanbag chairs and letting out long awkward sighs. I don't make eye contact with any of the other girls. I just want to wait for Amaya to become available. She's the only one I feel would actually work out.

DJ Tanner sits down in the beanbag chair next to me and says, "That was pretty fucked up."

I look over at him. He leans back in the seat that was previously occupied by the large bearded man, staring at me through dark Oakley lenses.

"Huh?" I ask him.

"What you said," he explains. "That's fucked up how you killed your wife."

I nearly fall off of my chair when he says that. "I didn't kill my wife."

He shrugs. "Sounds like you did to me. You shouldn't have been texting her while she was driving. She never would have been killed."

"She wasn't driving while she was texting. She was parked on the side of the road. A drunk driver lost control and hit her."

"Same thing," he says.

The kid is beginning to piss me off.

"It's not the same thing at all," I say.

"All I'm saying is if you weren't texting her she'd still be alive. If I had a sweet honey like your wife I wouldn't have left her alone on the side of the road to get hit by a drunk driver."

I raise my voice. "Sweet honey? You didn't know her. You weren't there."

"Relax, bro. I'm just making small talk."

"You call that small talk? You're blaming me for my wife's death. Don't you think I feel guilty enough?"

"Sorry, bro. I didn't realize you were that sensitive about it."

"It happened only three months ago. Of course I'm still sensitive."

He shrugs. "Three months is a long time. I've had five serious relationships in the past three months and have already moved on from all of them."

"How serious could they possibly be? I was with my

wife for almost two decades."

He shrugs again and taps his foot on the floor as if listening to a groovy reggae song in his head. "You'd be surprised. I love fast and hard, bro."

I shake my head, not sure what the hell this guy's problem is.

There's an awkward pause for a moment and then DJ Tanner says, "So do you want to snuggle or what?"

"Huh?" I ask, completely thrown off by the request.

"I'm asking if you want to snuggle. It's a cuddle party, isn't it?"

"Are you fucking serious?" I ask.

He nods. "I'm *always* serious."

"No, I don't want to snuggle with you."

"Why not? Is it because I'm a guy? I'm totally cool with snuggling other guys. It's not gay or anything."

I raise my eyebrows so high on my forehead that my eyes turn red. "It's not just because you're a guy. It's not even because I think you're an absolute prick. I just don't want to snuggle with you. You're not the right person, okay? Is that cool with you?"

He snorts and rubs his nose, then shrugs again.

"It's cool," he says, acting all rejected. "Whatever. I can snuggle anyone I want to." He stands up and looks away from me, his voice growing soft. "My snuggles are dope."

By the time Amaya finishes snuggling the first man, another guy is already jumping up to take his place. And after him, the big bearded guy steps in. It's like she's willing to snuggle with absolutely anyone who asks. This is a good thing and a bad thing for me. It's a good thing because she'll certainly be willing to snuggle with me, too. But it's bad because she might be preoccupied until the end of the session.

I'm worried the other girls might ask me to cuddle while I wait for Amaya, but none of them have tried to approach any of the men yet. Edna, the young girl with serious esteem issues, hasn't moved from her spot the entire time I've been here. She just stares at her hands, too awkward to ask anyone to cuddle. But she keeps sneaking peeks at me when she thinks I'm not looking. I wonder if she's waiting for me to approach her. God, I hope not. Worse would be if she's already coming up with a back story for me in her head. She's probably thinking up some crazy fantasy where I'm some successful celebrity lawyer and she's a barista at a late-night coffee house that I frequent, going over cases on my way home from the office. After she pours coffee in my lap and we catch each others' eyes, we instantly fall in love and throw ourselves into an epic romance the likes of which no one has experienced before…That would be creepy as hell.

I wait until Amaya is finished with Dan before approaching her. She seems to be relaxed and happy, as if the cuddle party is working out well for her. I feel like kind of an asshole cutting her off on her way to the bathroom, but I worry that if I don't I'll never get another opportunity.

She doesn't seem the least bit surprised when I step in front of her, as though she was expecting me to ask her. Maybe she was even hoping it would happen.

A bright smile lights up her face when our eyes meet. This is going to be a lot easier than I thought it would. I assumed it would be awkward as hell to ask somebody to snuggle with me. I thought it would make me feel like an utter creep. But the welcoming expression on her face puts me completely at ease.

"Would you be interested in cuddling with me?" I ask. Then I point to the bathroom behind us. "You know, after you get back."

She smiles at me and says, "No."

Her answer throws me off. The way she was looking at me I thought for sure she wanted to. She didn't turn down anyone who asked before me, not even the fat beardy guy.

"Really? Why?" I raise my voice in such a way that I startle even myself. It must have come across as way too aggressive.

She shakes her head. "Never ask anyone to explain their rejection to you. It's against the rules. When making a request for cuddles, just ask and accept whatever answer you get without pushing the issue. And when responding to an offer, just reply *yes* or *no* and leave it at that."

I nod my head and break eye contact, feeling even stupider that I asked.

But Amaya is patient and understanding. She takes my hand and squeezes it, then looks me in the eyes. "I'm sorry for your loss. I know exactly how you feel. I was there, too, not long ago. But it'll get better. I promise."

I'm happy that she's trying to console me, but I'm still confused about why I was rejected. She must understand how it feels to be in my shoes.

Almost as though she read my mind, Amaya explains, "No offense, it's just that you're too small to cuddle with me. My boyfriend was tall and muscular. It wouldn't do anything for me if I can't pretend that I'm cuddling with him." She lets go of my hand and works her way around me. "I have nothing against short guys, it's just the fantasy doesn't work if I stray too far away from his body type."

I nod my head and let her continue on her way to the bathroom, feeling stupid I asked. But I agree with her. Even if she agreed, the fantasy wouldn't have worked for me either. Julie was tall and curvy. Amaya is short and skinny like me. Our bodies wouldn't fit together right. I have to find somebody else.

Looking around the room, I have no idea who else to snuggle with. I was hoping to avoid all of the other women at the cuddle party. But I have no other choice. It's either try another partner or wait in the corner until it's time to go home.

When I notice Edna stealing glances again, I decide to

approach her. She's the person I'm most weirded out by of everyone in the room, but she seems the most available. Nobody has asked her to cuddle and it appears as though she's been waiting around for me to ask her the whole time.

But before I even ask her to cuddle, Edna just shakes her head and says, "No."

Then she goes back to looking at her hands.

What? Even Edna won't snuggle me? I thought she was dying for somebody to ask her. Was I mistaken about that? Maybe she wasn't stealing glances because she wanted me to ask her, perhaps she was dreading that I would.

I make sure not to ask her why she rejected me. After what happened with Amaya, I know to follow the rules and just walk away.

The next person I approach is Helen, the older woman. She has just finished snuggling with one of the other guys and is ready for more.

"That was amazing!" she yells out to the whole group, and then adds, "Who's next?" with her arms wide open, giggling with anticipation.

There are no takers so I decide to step in. "I'll cuddle with you."

Helen smiles and nods her head. "Then let's get to it, buckaroo! I don't have all day!"

I step toward her, straightening my pajamas and suddenly notice an old toothpaste stain at the bottom of my shirt. It seems everyone else is wearing fresh new pajamas that they probably purchased specifically for cuddle parties. I probably should have thought about that before coming. Wearing the same raggedy plaid pajamas I've been sleeping in for the past four years is pretty darned gross, even though I washed them the night before. Perhaps that's the reason Edna rejected me. She seems like the kind of person who would be anal about that sort of thing.

Covering the stain on my pajamas with my hand, I step closer to Helen, feeling more awkward than ever. I've not held anyone besides Julie for so long that it doesn't feel right touching another person. I don't even remember what it's like to touch a person in such a way for the first time. But I realize that Helen is probably the best choice of everyone in the room. Because of her age and positive demeanor, she seems safe. I can trust her. Even though her body shape is so much different from Julie's, she's probably the best choice for my first time.

Helen looks me up and down as though she's only just now noticed how small I am compared to the other guys.

"So are you a big spoon or a little spoon?" she asks.

"Little spoon," I say. "I'm probably too small to be big spoon."

Helen steps back and waves her hand. "Nevermind then. Maybe I'm old fashioned, but I think girls should always be the little spoon."

I shrug. "I can try big spoon, I guess…"

But Helen shakes her head. "Don't worry about it. I'll just cuddle with somebody else." And then goes to the back of the room for a cup of water.

I guess I don't really have many other options left.

As I scan the room, my eyes meet with DJ Tanner's and he says, "Don't look at me, bro. You lost your chance." Even though I had no intention of asking him.

Cherry calls out to the room and says, "Ten minutes left! Time for the puppy pile!"

I guess that's it. The session is about to end. I had to endure this terrible experience and never even got to cuddle with anyone. All I wanted to do was try it to see if it would help, but I didn't even get a chance to try. All I want to do is go home and lie in bed and forget any of this ever happened.

The puppy pile is where everyone in the room comes together into one giant bundle of snuggliness. I guess it's a tradition at Cuddle Me! to end each session with a big puppy pile, kind of like the grand finale at the end of a fireworks display.

I'm kind of grossed out by witnessing it. Everyone in the room participates except for me. DJ Tanner, Edna, Amaya, the whole lot of them, using each other's butts as pillows and hugging each other with both their arms and legs, purring and cooing and giggling at each other.

"Snuggles! Snuggles! Snuggles!" they all cry in cute cartoon voices.

It makes me feel sick.

Being the only person not participating is almost as awkward as being in the pile with them, but there's no way I'm joining in. I think I'll just wait until Cherry unlocks the door and lets us out.

Fourth Rule of Snuggle Club:

Although farting is both a natural and frequent occurrence in Snuggle Club, please ask your partner permission beforehand when possible.

CHAPTER
FOUR

Giving up on the cuddle party, I decide I might as well put my clothes back on and get ready to leave. But the second I turn toward the changing room, somebody leaps into my path. It's Melody, the scared woman who was crying in the bathroom earlier. I thought I was the only one who didn't join the puppy pile, but it makes sense that she wouldn't have felt comfortable with it either. I haven't seen her since the introductions and assumed she went back into the changing rooms to cry in a stall again, but maybe she's been hiding in the background the whole time and I never noticed.

"Would you cuddle with me?" Melody asks.

I'm thrown off by her request. I assumed she'd be the last person to ask me.

The only response that comes out of my mouth is, "What? Why?"

She looks away and says, "Nevermind. Forget I asked."

I shake my head. "I'm not saying no. I was just surprised you asked me."

"I heard you say that you like to be little spoon,"

Melody explains. "I need a partner who's okay with being little spoon."

I nod my head. "Yeah, my wife was taller than me so she was always big spoon."

She continues without acknowledging my explanation, "I don't like being little spoon because I'm uncomfortable with someone wrapping their arms around me. I feel trapped. I have to be the one who controls how close we touch and have the freedom to back off whenever I need to."

"I understand." I soften my voice for her as if trying to sound as harmless as possible.

She leads me to the other side of the room, about twenty feet away from the edge of the puppy pile. The area is lined with cushions and fluffy body pillows.

"Okay," she says. "Lay down. I'll join you when I feel ready."

I do as she says, kneeling down on the floor and reaching for a pink body pillow to cushion my head and elbow. I get as comfortable as I can in the yoga studio setting and wait for Melody to spoon me. The experience is far more nerve-wracking than I already expected, especially because it's with the traumatized girl of all people. I'm more worried about her than I am for myself, more focused on upsetting her than imagining that I'm cuddling with Julie once again.

But my worries fade and I just relax, taking deep breaths, trying to trick my brain into thinking that I'm at home in bed waiting for Julie to come under the covers with me. I close my eyes and prepare myself for her embrace, trying to hold myself back from crying. A few minutes pass and Melody is still standing there. Five more minutes and I'm still just lying on the ground waiting. She's not doing anything. I wonder if she got scared and left the room. I don't hear her breathing or moving. It's like she just left me here. All the other people in the room are probably watching me, wondering what the hell I'm doing snuggling all by myself.

Just as I decide to give up and leave my position, I feel Melody kneel down on the mat next to me and hover over my shoulders. Her long messy hair tickles my cheek and forehead. I decide not to move from my spot. I don't even open my eyes.

It takes her a few more minutes of hesitation, inching closer to me and reaching out her hands, but she still doesn't touch me. She seems terrified. I can feel her heavy breaths against the back of my neck, hear the sniffling of her nostrils. The closer she gets the more my muscles tense.

The cuddle party will likely be over by the time she actually touches me. I wonder if she'll ever build up the courage to go for it.

But right when it seems like she's going to pull away and give up, she drops down on the mat and wraps her left arm around me. I wouldn't exactly call it a snuggle. It's more like she's just lying on the ground next to me while resting her arm on top of mine. It's not comforting or cuddly at all. It's just dead weight.

I think this cuddle party was a bad idea. Melody is just too different from Julie. Even though they are about the same height, Melody feels nothing like her. I might as well have snuggled with a department store mannequin.

I just lie here for a while not sure what to do. It would be rude to ask her to get off of me. She's already scared enough. But the cuddle party doesn't seem to be ending. Cherry said ten more minutes at least ten minutes ago. Perhaps the puppy pile is going so well that none of them want it to end.

Melody relaxes a little and cuddles in closer. She puts her arm underneath mine and presses the palm of her hand against my chest. Her muscles sink into mine and her breaths ease into a rhythmic flow.

The cuddle is still awkward but gets better with each passing moment as the woman's comfort level increases. She rests her cheek against my shoulder and then folds my fingers into hers.

It all seems to be going perfectly well until she starts crying. Just a little at first—just a little sniffle here and there, a single tear wetting my pajamas. But her weeping grows. It vibrates through my whole body, tears pour down her cheeks onto mine.

"Are you okay?" I ask.

But she doesn't answer. She just keeps crying on me. Everyone in the room is looking at us, wondering what the hell is going on. I panic. I'm positive the others are going to blame me for her mental state. They're going to think I did something to upset her.

I try to wiggle my way out of the snuggle, but the second I move she grips tighter. She squeezes against me as tight as she can, moving her moist cheek against my neck and wailing into my ear. All the wind is being squished out of me. She locks her legs around mine. I'm not sure why she won't let me go. If cuddling me is causing her so much distress why won't she stop?

The two facilitators, Cherry and Dan, break out of the puppy pile and rush toward us. Cherry looks down into our faces with a concerned look.

"Are you alright, Melody?" she asks.

But Melody doesn't respond. She just keeps crying.

"Something's wrong," I cry out. "She's crushing my ribs!"

But Cherry doesn't seem very concerned for my wellbeing. She says, "Crying is a perfectly normal part of cuddling. It is both healthy and encouraged."

I endure the squishing for a few more minutes before Melody finally speaks.

She says, "He's…. he's…."

Cherry and Dan lean forward, waiting for an explanation with bated breaths.

"He's… he's…"

She crushes another rib and flexes her knees around my thigh.

"He's so snuggly!" Melody cries.

Then she lets out the rest of her tears and nuzzles her face into the back of my pajamas.

"He's the snuggliest person I've snuggled! I want to

snuggle him forever!" She squeezes my belly like a teddy bear's. "Please let me snuggle him forever!"

And then her cries turn to laughter and her laughter turns to sighs.

I don't have any idea what she's talking about. The snuggle isn't terrible but it's nothing to get emotional over. It's not even half as good as the worst snuggle I've ever had with Julie.

Cherry and Dan look at each other. Then they look down at me.

"He's that good, is he?" Cherry asks.

Melody just nods and snorts.

Cherry and Dan look at each other again.

"Maybe he's the one…" Dan says.

Cherry nods. "Only one way to find out."

The cuddle party facilitator gently pries Melody off of me. The woman fights it at first, but then relaxes and rolls away to another part of the mat. She just lies on her back, contented, basking in the glow of her cuddle session with me.

Even though the rule is to ask for permission before cuddling, Cherry is too impatient to deal with formalities. She lies down on the mat and lunges at me, wrapping herself around me and pressing me to her body.

"Huh…" she says, rubbing me like she's just tasted a fine wine and is swishing it around on her palate. "Yes. This is very nice." She holds me tighter, laying her head on me. "This is very nice indeed."

All the other cuddle party attendees gather around, watching the facilitator snuggle me.

After a few awkward minutes, Cherry explodes into emotion. "Oh my god! He's so snuggly!"

She giggles out loud and hugs me tighter.

"He's so soft!" she cries. "He's like a little teddy bear! I want to snuggle him forever!"

She quickly becomes way too aggressive and squeezes me even tighter than Melody was.

"Is he the one?" Dan asks her.

"Yes! Yes! Yes!" Cherry nuzzles her chin against my arm. "He's the one! He's the one we've been waiting for!"

Dan strokes his beard and nods. Then he says, "Let me try."

Cherry releases me with much more willingness than the last girl. She rolls over and lies down next to Melody with a crazy smile on her face. The other people in the group look at each other, snickering, amazed by what they're seeing.

Dan lies down next to me and wraps his large beefy arm around me.

"I'm not cool with this," I tell them.

But Dan doesn't listen.

"I'll only be a minute," he says in his deep gruff voice.

I've never been snuggled by a man before. It's much, much different than being with Julie. His weight is heavy and his grunts are intense. I feel his beard tickling my neck as he cozies himself against me and says, "Yes. Yes, this is divine. Like nothing I've experienced."

"What the hell are you doing to me?" I cry as I feel something stabbing into my back.

"I can feel your aura seeping into me," he whispers

into my ear. "You have a very sensual essence."

I realize the thing stabbing me in the back is his penis. The bearded guy is growing a massive boner and it's pressed right up against my spine.

"I feel it!" I cry. "It's touching me!"

As I yell, Cherry jumps up and goes to me. Instead of breaking us apart, she leans down and strokes my hair.

"Don't worry about it," she says, knowing exactly what I'm complaining about. "Erections are a perfectly natural part of snuggling. They're nothing to be scared of."

The only thing I can think of to respond to that is, "What the fuck!"

But before I need to struggle my way out of Dan's grip, he releases me and lets me get to my feet. Then everyone in the room applauds.

What the hell was that? What the hell is wrong with these people?

Cherry, Dan, and Melody approach me. All of them nod their heads.

"That was amazing," they all say in unison.

Fifth Rule of Snuggle Club:

It's inappropriate to tease, insult or compliment another person's boner at Snuggle Club.

CHAPTER
FIVE

As the cuddle party comes to a close, everyone returns to the changing room and puts their everyday clothes back on. They all chat and laugh with each other, seeming refreshed from another successful snuggle session. But I don't feel very refreshed. I feel kind of molested and freaked out. I want to shower all of these people off of me and block the whole experience from my memory. I hoped it would help me relax and maybe even get some sleep finally, but after this, I don't know if I'll ever sleep again.

Melody is back to crying in the changing room as I enter to retrieve my clothes, only she now seems to be crying with joy.

When Melody sees me, she says, "Thank you. You have no idea how much that helped me."

I just nod and wave, not sure how else to respond. All I did was lie there and let people have their way with me. I'm glad I helped her, but I kind of wish it never happened.

Looking around the changing room, I can't find my backpack with my clothes anywhere. It's not in the place I left it. Because there aren't any lockers, none of our stuff was secure back here. Anyone could have snagged it. Perhaps somebody mistook it for their own and moved it somewhere.

Many of the other snugglers are completely dressed and leaving the changing room, but none of them have my bag in tow.

Out in the main room, Cherry has unlocked the entrance and is allowing people to leave. She hugs Edna, Amaya, and Helen goodbye. She high-fives the guys who just came in to creep on women. When DJ Tanner is about to leave, he looks back at me and then at Cherry.

"He's not *that* good at snuggling is he?" DJ Tanner asks her.

She smiles and nods at him, "Oh, yes… He's something special."

DJ Tanner sneers. "He can't be better than *me*. I'm the best snuggler in town."

Cherry politely ignores him.

"Everyone wants to snuggle with me…" he says. His voice grows soft as though he realizes he's not fooling anyone. I don't think he cuddled a single person at the cuddle party.

When DJ Tanner leaves, Cherry locks the door behind him and hides the key in her pocket. Dan comes in behind me, leaving me trapped between them.

Cherry looks in my direction and says, "We want you to stay behind. There's so much we have to talk to you about."

I step to my side, trying not to get cornered by the weird cuddle people.

"Where's my stuff?" I ask them. "I couldn't find my backpack anywhere."

Dan says, "We'll return your belongings soon enough. But first, you have to hear us out."

"Hear you out? You're not going to try to snuggle me again are you?"

Cherry shakes her head. "We would never do that. You don't have to snuggle anyone you don't want to."

After what just happened, I don't know if I believe her.

Dan steps in, "We belong to a group of elite snuggle enthusiasts. The best snugglers in the world. We'd like you to join our ranks."

"We call it the Snuggle Club," Cherry says.

"Wasn't this the Snuggle Club?" I ask, continuing to back up.

They shake their heads.

"Cuddle parties are a minor diversion for amateur snugglers," Cherry says. "The Snuggle Club only recruits the best and we think you have what it takes to join the inner circle."

I laugh out loud. "Are you fucking kidding me?"

Dan grunts. "We are not kidding at all. We take snuggling very seriously."

"I can tell…" I say.

Cherry realizes my unease and steps between Dan and I. "I'm sorry if we seem so forward. We're just really passionate about our work. We've been looking for someone like you for a long time." She goes to me and takes my hands, looks me straight in the eyes. "You're something very special, Ray. Only one in ten million people possess such a marvelous gift. I just want to help you understand how wonderful you are."

Tears fill her eyes, melting her clownish makeup. The fact that she's getting so emotional only makes me worry even more. I step around them, heading toward the changing rooms. I wonder if I can lock myself in and escape through a window.

But before I can get into the next room, Melody steps through the doorway and blocks my path. She says, "It's okay, Ray. Nobody's going to hurt you."

She's with them? I thought she was just another random person at the cuddle party. She's the last person I'd expect to be part of the *inner circle* or whatever the hell their group is called.

"We just want you to come to one encounter," Cherry says. "Just one. If you don't like it we'll never bother you again."

"I still don't understand what you're talking about," I say.

Dan explains, "We want you to attend one Snuggle Club meeting. The next one is here tonight, right now. We want you to stay for it. We want to introduce you to the rest of the inner circle."

I shake my head. "No, thank you. I don't want to stay. I need to get home."

I push past them and rush for the exit. I jiggle the door handle, but it won't open. I slam my fist against it and call out for help. There are people outside leaving the California Pizza Kitchen, but they don't seem to hear me. The whole room appears to be soundproofed.

"What do you have to go home to, Ray?" Cherry asks me.

I look back.

"An empty house?" she asks. "A cold bed? Your wife's gone and never coming back. You'll never get to snuggle with her again."

She comes to me and puts her hands on my shoulders.

"But you can snuggle with us. We want you to be a part of our family. We want you to find a place where you belong."

Then she hugs me and all my muscles are tranquilized. There's something powerful in her embrace. My body feels soothed and sedated. Her touch calms me, makes me no longer interested in fleeing. Cherry has a power that I didn't realize. She, too, is a magnificent snuggler. I wonder why she hasn't used this gift before. She didn't feel like this when she cuddled me earlier. I wonder if Cherry reserves this snuggle-skill for special occasions, only when it's needed most.

Without releasing me from her calming embrace, she asks, "Won't you just try spending one night with us? Just one night?"

Her flesh purrs around me, pacifying me. I feel like I can fall asleep in her grasp. It's been so long since I've slept, *really* slept. Perhaps this is what I've been looking for, what I've been needing. It's almost like a drug.

Before I can stop myself, I say, "Okay. I'll give it a shot."

Then she drops me. "Excellent! Everyone will be so thrilled!"

I fall to the ground and slope back against the door. It's like I've just been hit by a garbage truck made of pillows and cotton candy. As I drift in and out of consciousness, I wonder what exactly I've gotten myself into. Nothing good can possibly come from getting involved with these crazy cuddle-obsessed people.

Sixth Rule of
Snuggle Club:

Pretending your partner is a giant marshmallow is perfectly acceptable at Snuggle Club… as long as you don't attempt to eat their head.

CHAPTER
SIX

Once I recompose myself, I get to my feet and look around the room. It seems as though some time has passed since I left Cherry's embrace. Did I fall asleep? I'm not sure. I wouldn't be surprised if I did.

Melody, Cherry, and Dan have all changed their clothes and are now wearing matching outfits—these weird black silk robes. Cherry comes to me and drops another one in my lap.

"Put this on," she says. "It's what we all wear in the inner circle."

I lift it up and examine the robe. It's very soft. Softer than any fabric I've ever felt in my life. When I first saw it, I wanted to throw it on the ground and refuse to wear such a ridiculous thing, but now that I'm holding it I want nothing more than to put it on and feel it against my body.

"This is so soft…" I say, rubbing it against my face.

Cherry nods. "It's made from the finest oggderian silk. Nothing is more comfortable on Earth or any planet for that matter. Very few people have ever had the honor of wearing such a heavenly garment. You should feel blessed."

I have no idea what she's talking about, but I can't wait to get it on. I rush to the changing room and rip off my pajamas. The moment I pull the robe over me, my naked skin feels soothed and massaged by its comfort. I wish I had an entire wardrobe made of this material. I wish all of my sheets and blankets were this preternaturally soft.

When I leave the changing room, the other three are waiting for me. They smile with satisfaction to see me in the garment, nodding at how well it suits me.

Although the whole thing seems creepier than ever, I still find myself excited to snuggle again. This garment fills me not only with comfort but with anticipation.

"When will the others arrive?" I ask them.

They look at me confused.

"Others?" Dan asks.

"Ummm…" I say, wondering why it was such an odd question. "The other members of the Snuggle Club?"

I'm beginning to wonder if it's just going to be the four of us. I assumed it was a large group of people showing up, not just them.

When Cherry understands my confusion, she nods and says, "They're not coming to us. We're going to them."

We're leaving the Cuddle Me! shop? Why did we put on these robes now if we're going to another location?

The three of them pull the yoga mats off the floor and move them to the sides of the room, revealing a trap door on the ground. It's a massive flap made of iron and wood, like the kind of entrance one would find leading to a medieval dungeon.

"They're waiting for us," Cherry says.

Dan and Melody pull on the iron handles and lift the heavy doors to reveal a staircase leading down into the dark.

Was this always here? We're in a strip mall, in a building that was obviously once a yoga studio. Why is there a basement here? How the hell did they get the zoning to build such a thing?

"Hold on just a moment," Cherry tells me. "We just need to prepare everyone for a newcomer."

Then she and Dan descend into the darkness.

What the hell is going on? Are there actually people down there? Have they been down in the basement this whole time?

A part of me is worried that they have people held hostage down there. People they've liked cuddling so much at the cuddle party that they lock them down inside of a snuggle dungeon and never let them leave. It's beginning to freak the hell out of me.

Melody doesn't go down there with them. She comes to me and puts her hand on my shoulder.

"I want to thank you again for what you did for me," she says. "I haven't been able to participate in the inner circle workings for so long that I thought I would never be able to return. But it's such an important part of my life. I've cried almost every day since the attack.

Not just because it was such a horrible experience, but also because it scared me away from my family. I couldn't handle to be touched by anyone. Now I think I'm ready to return."

She hugs me without hesitation or tension, just wrapping her arms around me and resting her head in the crook of my neck.

"I feel like I'm whole again," she says.

As she holds me, I feel the robes around us swell and glow, amplifying the comfort of her embrace. It feels wonderful. Not as wonderful as hugging Julie, but wonderful in another way. A magical way.

Still timid about the whole situation, I ask Melody, "Are there really people down there? Who are they? Are they being held prisoner?"

Melody snickers and pushes away from me.

"No, no…" she says. "The rest of the inner circle are very serious about snuggling. They stay down there for days or weeks at a time, practicing their artform. They are very serious about it. Much more so than the rest of us. I only wish I could be so dedicated to the club."

"Don't they have jobs or families to go to?" I ask. "Don't they have lives outside of snuggling?"

Melody thinks about it, then answers, "Well, the leaders of the inner circle are independently wealthy. They provide for any snuggler worthy enough to join their ranks. You don't have to have a job if you don't want to. You can quit your job, sell your house, and snuggle full time for the rest of your life if that's what you choose to do. They will keep you fed and happy. You'll never have another care in the world."

I think about that for a moment. Although snuggling with Julie full time for the rest of our lives always sounded like a dream come true, I couldn't imagine doing that with anyone else. It kind of sounds like a complete nightmare.

"Why don't Dan and Cherry live down there with them?" I ask.

"Because they are recruiters," Melody says. "They're needed to find more people like you and me. Otherwise, they probably would stay down there on a more regular basis."

"And what about you? Would you stay down there for days at a time?"

Melody lowers her eyes and shrugs. "I don't know. Maybe if they'd let me. But I'm not a professional. I probably couldn't hack it. I can only dream of doing it fulltime." She turns away from me. "After the attack, I lost my drive. I was scared. I didn't feel worthy. I hope I can get that back…"

I nod my head. "I'm sorry about that. A close friend of mine was raped when I was in college. I don't think she ever quite recovered from it."

"Raped?" Melody asks, her voice changing to a defensive tone. "Do you think I was raped?"

I lift my arms and apologize for misspeaking.

"I never said I was raped," she says. "It wasn't that at all. I can't believe you."

I have no idea what else she could be talking about, but decide not to pry into it. I just say, "I'm sorry," and back off.

She quickly forgives my misstep and changes the subject. I guess she can't stay mad at me after whatever help she thinks I gave her.

"I didn't mean to snap at you," she says. "It's just a sensitive subject. In any case, I'm happy to be able to experience this session with you. Your whole life is about to change. You'll see. Everything will be better."

Dan returns by himself and calls us toward him. I didn't hear anything down there while we were waiting. No other people, no one speaking, I didn't even detect their footsteps as they descended into the dark.

"They're ready for you," he tells us.

Melody signals for me to go first. I'm not sure if it's because she's being polite or because they think I'll try to escape if I go last.

I know going down there is a terrible idea, but there's something I feel attracted to. Some kind of warm, comfortable energy that calms me. I can only describe it as the feeling I'd get whenever Julie embraced me, the loving energy that made me never want to let her go.

The force pulls me, drawing me toward it. I find myself willing to take the steps down into the dark underground. My brain tells me to run but my heart won't let me. It's like I'm entering the place where Julie's soul resides, as though I'll get to be with her if I just keep going.

As I follow Dan, he turns back and says, "You feel

it, don't you? Their auras? That's the power of the inner circle. Their snuggling spirit is so strong that you can feel it from this far away. You don't even have to cuddle with them to feel like you're in the best cuddle of your life. It's magic. Pure magic."

I can't believe I'm agreeing with the creepy hippy dude, but it's true. I feel like I'm in someone's loving embrace without even touching another human being.

Melody steps down and shuts the trapdoor behind us, enmeshing us in darkness. The door locks the instant it is closed, but it's not Melody's doing. The lock is automatic. A part of me is terrified that I'm now trapped and unable to escape, but another part, the part that is powerless to this feeling that overwhelms me, doesn't care in the slightest bit.

At the bottom of the steps, my eyes adjust to the darkness and I realize that it's not completely without light. There's a pleasant green glow all around us, issuing from the walls. I can't exactly pinpoint where the light is coming from or what kind of light it even is, but it's made me capable of seeing perfectly fine. It's actually very pleasing to the eye, calming. The perfect light for a snuggle session.

As we traverse a dimly lit passageway, I realize this isn't just a basement. It's a labyrinth of underground catacombs that must stretch not only past the Cuddle Me! storefront, but the entire strip mall above. How long has this underground passage been here? It seems old, far older than the mall that was built on top of it. Maybe even older than the whole city.

After several minutes of walking, Dan says, "It's still a bit farther. But it's worth the walk. You'll see."

The stone ground should be cold on my bare feet, but it's not for some reason. It's warm and soothing, like one of those fancy heated tile bathroom floors.

The closer we get to the inner circle, the more I feel that loving embrace. It beckons to me, urging me to come to it. No matter how crazy it seems, I must see this thing through to the end. It's far too late for me to back out now.

Seventh Rule of Snuggle Club:

Telepathic snuggles are strictly reserved for platinum card-carrying members of Snuggle Club. It is prohibited to use these powers in public, not even to pacify violent criminals or impress chicks at bars.

CHAPTER
SEVEN

We arrive at a large room three times the size of the Cuddle Me! storefront. Large, but still comfortably intimate. The floor here is soft and pillowy against my feet. It's nothing like the horrible yoga mats upstairs. The entire ground seems to be like a giant mattress, only a thousand times more comfortable than a normal mattress. The more I walk on it, the more amazing it feels. Even more amazing than the robe I wear. It's like I'm walking on a cloud, walking on a rainbow.

On the far side of the room, Cherry waits for us with a group of other robed figures. They all stand very still, like shadows. I don't see their eyes or even their faces, but I can tell they are staring at us, probably excited to meet the newcomer. If I'm so good at snuggling, of course they'd want to meet me, wouldn't they?

But once we arrive, not a single one acknowledges my presence. They appear to be in some kind of trance, absorbing the snuggly energy around them.

Cherry is the only one who acknowledges us.

"Welcome…" She nods in our direction, then turns

to the others. "Brothers and sisters, I'd like to introduce you to a neophyte in our ranks. Please welcome Brother Ray with a snuggle."

I step back, worried that the horde of robed shadow people are about to attack me with a group hug. But they don't snuggle me with their bodies. They snuggle me with their minds. A wave of warm love fills my whole being, infusing me with peace and contentment. I've never felt anything like it. These people truly are masters of the art of snuggling. I now completely understand Dan's hippy talk of auras and the spiritual embrace. Perhaps he's much wiser than I've given him credit for.

"And I'd like you to also welcome back Sister Melody," Cherry continues. "She has finally overcome the afflictions that have kept her from our side, all thanks to the natural talent of Brother Ray."

As Melody pulses with the spiritual love of the inner circle, it begins to dawn on me just how seriously fucked up all of this is. Are people really snuggling me with their minds? How the fuck is any of this real? I'm beginning to think Cherry somehow injected me with some kind of drug that is causing me to hallucinate all of this.

But even if that's the case, I'm loving the sensation. I can't wait to see where this goes next.

They don't bother with introductions as they did at the cuddle party upstairs, which is kind of a shame. I'm pretty interested in learning who these strange fulltime snugglers are and what they're all about, especially if I'm supposed to be snuggling with them later. But even though we're skipping the formalities, we don't go straight into the cuddle session. Cherry has some things she wants to tell us, mostly for my sake.

We all sit down on the pillowy ground and fold our legs, listening to her words.

Cherry says, "Most people are unaware of the magic that a snuggle holds. It's a secret, powerful enchantment that only the gifted few truly understand. We elite snugglers are in tune with this power and use it to benefit those we serve—the great saviors beyond the veil. They are the masters of the art of snuggling and we are humbled to receive them into our world. Although we possess small, lowly snuggle abilities, we are nothing compared to their greatness. We can do naught but serve and obey, for they are the shining light that illuminates our meager existence."

It suddenly dawns on me that I've just joined a crazy snuggle cult, but for some reason, I don't really mind all that much. Yeah, these people are even weirder than I thought and I don't understand a single word Cherry is muttering, but it still feels good to be here. I've never felt more relaxed in my whole life.

No longer able to follow Cherry's babble, I look around the room at the other people in the cult. Melody is crying again, she cries tears of joy, ecstatic to be welcomed back into the fold. But it's not just her, Dan is crying as well and Cherry is crying between words as she speaks. But the other people don't appear to be as moved. I examine them more closely, trying to make out their profiles, but something's odd about most of them. Their faces look distorted and melted. It's probably just the dim lighting, but one of them seems to have his eyes and nose on the side of his face instead of the front. Another one seems to have a face on her neck instead of her head. It's as if their facial features have been smudged, like a drawing that was poorly erased.

Cherry concludes her speech with, "Our power will fuel the world with love and positivity. Without our snuggles, the darkness would surely overwhelm the Earth."

I still have no idea what the hell she was talking about, but I'm glad it's over. Dan and Melody are the only ones to clap for her. The others just continue sitting and staring forward. A part of me wonders if they're even real. Perhaps they are just statues or mannequins. I thought I saw them move, I'm positive they have moved at least a little. But are they real?

When Cherry tells the group, "Form the Circle of Welcoming," I realize that I wasn't mistaken. The other people are actually capable of moving.

Everyone forms a circle, spreading apart about three feet away from each other. I sit between Melody and Dan. Cherry sits on the opposite side of the circle.

When we are all in position, Cherry asks, "Is everyone

ready? I can feel them on the other side waiting for us. Let's give it everything we've got."

I have no idea what's going on, but suddenly everyone around me becomes very serious. All of them concentrate, their focus pointed at the center of the circle.

I lean over to Melody and ask, "What the hell is going on?"

But she doesn't respond, too busy concentrating.

Dan is the one to explain it to me, "We're trying to open the gate to the Snuggleverse."

"The what?" I can't help but laugh at him.

"Just stare at the center of the circle and concentrate. Push all of your snuggle energy toward it. Imagine that space is your departed wife and you're wrapping your body around her, filling her with your spiritual power."

I look at the center of the circle and back at Dan. Then I shrug and say, "Sure, if you say so. I'll give it a shot."

Why not? How could it possibly get any weirder than this?

I do exactly as he says, pushing my aura toward the center of the circle. I imagine that the air is an invisible figure, Julie's figure. I imagine that I'm reaching my arms around her and pulling it to my chest. But nothing seems to happen. I don't feel anything. It's not the same as when the inner circle snuggled me with their mind.

But then I remember that I'm normally a little spoon, not a big spoon. I wouldn't push my snuggle toward Julie, I would pull her around me like I would a blanket on a cold night. So I imagine the center of the room is my wife ready to hold me and pull its arms forward, around

79

my back, spooning me tightly to her.

The moment I imagine this, a bright blue light fills the room. It opens up like a slit in the air, widening to let in even more of the brilliant glow.

"It's working!" Cherry cries. "It's really working!"

"I knew you were the one," Dan tells me. "I knew your power would open the gate."

"The gate?" I ask. "That's a gate?"

Tears fall down Melody's cheeks as she adds, "I never thought this would happen again! It's so beautiful!"

Dan says, "We haven't been able to open the gate for a couple of years now. Our powers weren't strong enough. But you changed that. You joined our ranks at just the right time."

"I did what now?" I ask.

But Dan's attention diverts from me to the gateway. Once it opens wide enough for a person to pass through, everyone in the room bows their heads all the way to the floor, waiting to greet the gods of the Snuggleverse.

Dan's burly hand wraps around the back of my head and forces it to the floor, making me bow in the presence of the Great Snuggly Ones. All I can think is *what the fuck is this shit?* as an array of large fuzzy creatures bounce through the shining gate into the room with us.

There are plump balls of fluff the size of cows that bounce on tiny tentacle-like stalks. There are long spongy pink and orange-striped worm-like creatures that seem to float without gravity. There are bulbous furry cuddle monsters wobbling in with large mouths and long felt-tipped tongues that appear to be made of cloth. A dozen other creatures follow them, at least two of each kind. All of them look like massive stuffed animals that have somehow come to life. All of them are some kind of combination between cute and terrifying. And all of them appear to be absolutely, mind-numbingly snuggly.

"Behold, the Great Ones!" Cherry tells the group. She turns to the creatures. "You honor us with your snuggles!"

One of the cuddle monsters gurgles and coos at her, but it's in a language none of us understand. None of the other humans appear worried or scared of these things, but every single one fills me with unease. Their cotton-like eyes and plushy flesh make them look like horrific Sesame Street abominations, the ones that they no longer air on the show because they proved too terrifying to child viewers.

But, even though I find them all scary as hell, I can't help but grow the urge to snuggle each and every one of them. They are like the ultimate stuffed animals, the kind of thing I've dreamed about snuggling with ever since I was a little kid.

"Let the feast of snuggles commence!" Cherry calls out to the group.

And, as if they understand her, the creatures dig in, bouncing and slithering toward the cuddle cultists, choosing their partners with care.

When I arrived in the inner circle, I thought I'd be snuggling with the other members of the cult. But it's not that way at all. None of the humans are snuggling with other humans. They are all here to snuggle with these strange creatures.

I assume Cherry and Dan purposely withheld this information from me. They knew I would not have gone into the basement otherwise. I would have fought for my life to get the hell out of there as fast as I could and no locked door would've stopped me.

If it wasn't for the peaceful calm washing over me I would run now, but the light from the Snuggleverse is even more powerful than that of the inner circle. It's almost paralyzing. I can't get enough of it.

The other humans in the room are pairing off with different creatures from the gate. They don't get to choose who they're paired with, however. The creatures choose them. One of those weird fluffy worm things chooses Dan. It coils around him, wrapping him up like a boa constrictor and he oozes with bliss at the sensation. One of the floppy cuddle monsters goes after Melody. She cries as it embraces her. It snuggles her into its big fluffy chest and rolls them onto the ground, making burping, giggling noises.

It seems that Cherry is the only one who hasn't been chosen. She just stands there alone, nodding happily. Obviously disappointed, but still happy and content to be in the presence of her gods. I wonder if the Snuggleverse creatures are just as creeped out by her as us humans are.

I'm kind of jealous of Cherry, though. I wish I was left out of the choosing as she was. But I'm not so lucky. It's completely obvious which creature has chosen me, as one of the bouncing balls of fluff comes in my direction.

I realize the thing is actually more than a ball of fluff once it comes closer to me. It's more like one of those old troll dolls if its pink hair had grown so wild that it swallowed its whole body.

The thing comes right up to me and presses its soft cotton candy hair against my body. Then I swear it talks to me in a high-pitched cartoonish voice, only its tiny troll-like mouth doesn't move. It's like it speaks to me with its mind.

It says, "Snuggle me!"

And bounces on me with such force I fall to the cloud-like floor.

"Snuggle me!"

Little spongy limbs emerge from its fur and stretch around my body. I want to push it away and scream in its tiny face, but decide that might be a terrible idea. These things just want to snuggle. If I piss it off the weird furry thing might rip off my head.

So I just go with it. I wrap my arms around its fluff and relax against the pillowy ground. The thing is warm and beyond soft. It purrs at me, relaxing my mind to the point where I feel drugged. I've never done heroin before, but if I had I imagine this is what it would feel like.

Without a snuggle partner, Cherry comes to me to see how I'm doing. But she doesn't ask if I'd like to be separated from the strange creature. She just wants to hear me talk about how wonderful it feels, maybe so she could live vicariously through me.

"She's an oggderian," Cherry says, stroking its fur as it snuggles me. I have no idea how she knows it's a girl. "Isn't she soft? We weave our robes from their fur."

The creature's silky hide does feel a lot like the robe I'm wearing, but I didn't realize this until it was mentioned. Cherry gently pulls locks of hair from the creature and collects it into a pile. Scissors or shears are not needed to harvest the oggderian's fur. It comes out as easily as separating strands of cotton candy. The thing doesn't even seem to feel it.

As Cherry harvests the creature's coat, I ease into the snuggle. It's still not as good as snuggling with Julie. It's weird and unique, but still very relaxing. I enjoy it far more than the snuggle I had with Cherry or the one with Melody. But it just reminds me of how great it was to snuggle with my wife. Nothing will ever compare to what it was like to be with her.

The cultists say that I'm a very gifted snuggler, but it was really Julie who was the one that made our snuggles great. She was the queen of snuggles. She knew exactly how to make me feel warm and loved. If Julie was here with me now, she would blow away everyone in this room. The cultists, the creatures, none of them could hold a candle to her cuddles.

As my mind drifts off into memories of my departed wife, the oggderian begins to grow warmer, its purrs vibrate louder, its snuggles intensify.

"What's it doing?" I ask Cherry as the thing's vibrations become more and more furious.

Cherry shifts her attention from the fur to me. "Oh my... She really likes you…"

"Likes me?" I cry.

The thing shakes and quivers.

"You're making her so happy!" Cherry says.

Once the snuggle reaches a climax, the creature explodes into a spasm. Tiny balls of fluff pop out of its hide, rolling over my shoulders. The thing makes squeaky, sneezing noises with each ball that is released.

"What the hell?" I cry.

I look at one of the puffballs. It jiggles and shifts, trying to roll over onto its side. I think these things are alive.

"What are they?" I ask.

When Cherry sees them, her eyes light up with excitement.

"They're your babies!" she cries.

"My what?"

Then I see what she's saying. When the puffball rolls over, I notice it has the face of a human baby. Only it's the size of a golf ball. My expression contorts in horror as the thing lets out a high-pitched wail. Not just this puffball baby, but all of them. There must be twenty of the things twitching and shivering around us.

"Oggderians mate by snuggling," Cherry explains,

her voice beyond excited. "It's the same to them as sexual intercourse."

So this weird creature wasn't just snuggling me this whole time? It was mating with me?

Cherry says, "You should feel honored. You have produced offspring with a snuggle god!"

As I look around the room, I notice the same thing happening to two other cultists that are snuggling with oggderians. Tiny balls of fluff are popping out of their mates and piling up on the floor.

When Cherry notices all the baby puffballs, she becomes even more excited. "Oh my! I've never seen so many! Oggderians usually don't mate with humans. They just snuggle us for fun. There must be something about the energy you bring to our group that's making them extra fertile."

"Are you fucking serious?"

The puffballs wail and roll around in circles. I have no idea what the hell the half-human creatures will grow into, but I can't handle the idea that I brought them into this world just by snuggling with this weird thing. I try to break free from the monster's grasp, but Cherry stops me.

"Don't break the snuggles!" she warns. "Don't even move. You must keep cuddling for as long as the god wishes it. It's sacrilege to deny her your love."

I decide not to offend the weird creature and give in, allowing it to purr against my body. As long as it doesn't produce more offspring, I think I can endure it.

Eighth Rule of Snuggle Club:

If snuggling an oggderian female results in a brood of offspring, you are not permitted to take one home to keep as a pet.

CHAPTER
EIGHT

The oggderian doesn't seem interested in releasing me anytime soon. In fact, she appears to be digging in and preparing to go to sleep, ready to pass out in her mate's arms.

While she vibrates against my body, I look across the room at what the others are doing. Those with oggderians are in the same boat as me, falling asleep with their fluffy creatures after their strange mating session. But things are much different for those snuggling with the other types of creatures, especially those with the large worm-like things.

The worms snuggle much more fiercely than the oggderians. They are constantly squirming and coiling and squeezing their snuggle partners. It's almost as if they're trying to murder the humans instead of cuddle with them.

Dan is with one of these fuzzy worms, but the blissed-out look on his face tells me that it's not as painful as it appears. It's like he's getting a full body massage that is kneading his muscles into a superbly relaxed state.

But as I watch carefully, I realize something far more is happening to him than getting a mere massage. The creature is not just kneading his flesh. It seems to be molding it like clay. As the worm coils and squeezes around Dan's body, it transforms him into some kind of human putty. It molds his body, spreading it out and squishing it together. His facial features are smeared across the side of his head—his eyes where his cheek is supposed to be, his beard now a spiral in the center of his face—making him look like a painting of a man that's been splashed with water and left to melt down the side of the canvas.

"Those are the slingydings," Cherry tells me as I watch the worm distort Dan's flesh. "They are the sculptors of the Snuggleverse. They come to our world to shape us into beautiful works of art."

I wasn't imagining it when I saw the other cultists with distorted faces. They must have been snuggled by these creatures in the past, made into freaks by their transformative snuggles.

"But normally they don't work this fast," Cherry adds. "It usually takes multiple snuggle sessions to turn us into their completed works of art. I'm sure it's your powerful snuggle energy that is making this possible. You're like a muse to them, fueling their creative drive."

Some of the other cultists have been even more transformed than Dan. The ones who were already mutated before this snuggle session started are now unrecognizable as human beings. The slingydings have squished them into balls, folded their limbs into their torsos and shaped them into blob-like sculptures. I don't see their faces at all anymore. I don't even know if they can breathe in such a state.

If I'm the one who's causing all of this I couldn't feel more terrible about myself. These poor people are being squished into horrific works of art and there's nothing I can do about. For some reason, every single one of them seems to be enjoying the experience beyond words. That kind of makes me feel better about it. But, still, it's terrible. I'm thankful beyond words that I was chosen by an oggderian rather than a slingyding. I might have unintentionally produced offspring with a weird fuzzy creature, but at least I'm still in the same shape I arrived in.

I'm happy Melody is not in the same ship as Dan. The large cuddle monster that's wrapping itself around her might be the creepiest looking creature of the group—with its bulbous cotton eyes and long squishy tongue hanging from its massive Kermit the Frog mouth—but it seems to be the safest. It's not distorting her flesh or breeding with her. It just wants to cuddle like a nice cuddle monster should.

But just as I sigh with relief, the creature lifts Melody off the ground and lowers her into its massive foamy mouth.

I scream so loud the oggderian lying against me is stirred back into consciousness. "What the hell!"

But Cherry holds me down, stopping me from breaking the snuggle with my fluffy mate. I have no choice but to watch as the gargantuan muppet swallows the woman whole, gobbling her down gulp by gulp. The look on Melody's face isn't one of horror, but one of complete and utter happiness, like she's never wanted anything more in her life. After she goes down its throat, only her long messy blond hair remains dangling from its fuzzy mouth. It slurps up her hair like spaghetti and then lies back down on the floor, gripping its swollen stomach.

"It fucking ate her!" I cry. "It ate Melody!"

But Cherry doesn't express the same emotions as I do.

"That's the cuddlesaur," she explains. "They come to our world to feed on us. They rarely ever swallow anyone, though. They usually just absorb our snuggle energy. But your power must have made them much hungrier than usual. You gave them ravenous appetites. Snuggle energy alone wasn't enough to fill them."

When I look around the room, I realize all of the cuddlesaurs are lying with full bellies. They must have all eaten their snuggle partners already, now falling asleep to digest their meals.

Cherry stares longingly at the cuddlesaur bulge that once was Melody.

"I'm so jealous…" she cries. "Curled up inside of his big wet tummy must be the snuggliest snuggle ever. She must be so happy!"

I can't believe what the crazy bitch is saying. "Happy? It fucking ate her! She's going to die in there!"

Cherry just shakes her head at me and says, "Feeding

our gods is a great honor. Any one of us would gladly give our lives to satiate their appetites."

That's it. I've had enough of this weird ass cult. These creatures aren't here for snuggles. They don't care about us one bit. They're just here to eat us, mold us, and molest us. Nothing good could possibly come from staying here.

The large fluff ball releases me before I have to pull myself away from it. The thing hops to its spindly legs and returns to the gate. My little puffball children follow the creature like ducklings after their mother. None of them acknowledge me whatsoever and I'm perfectly fine with that. I hope I never see any of those things ever again.

It seems like the snuggle session has come to a close as other creatures exit through the gate. Not all of them, but the majority of them. Some linger behind. A couple slingydings are still busy sculpting their cuddle partners. A few cuddlesaurs are fast asleep after swallowing their human-sized meals.

But it's not over yet. Cherry pushes me back to the ground as I'm attempting to get to my feet.

"Something else is coming," she tells me.

I begin to panic. Was that just the first wave of cuddle creatures? Will a whole new batch enter and start the whole process over? Will there be even stranger breeds of monsters than the ones before? I really don't want to stay and find out.

It's not a new horde of creatures that comes through the portal. It's just one. A tall, pillowy woman-shaped creature. This is the only one that has resembled a human, but she's more like a cloth doll than a living being. She's made with different colored fabric. A patchwork girl. Her hair red and fluffy. Her eyes large and friendly. Her mouth is made of stitches. Her nipples made of buttons. It's like the Snuggleverse's version of Frankenstein's monster.

"Oh my god!" Cherry cries. Then she lowers her head and bows.

"What?" I ask.

"It's the Queen of the Snuggleverse," she explains. "She only appears in our world once every hundred years."

A hundred years? This freaky shit has been going on that long?

Everyone bows in the presence of the Snuggle Queen. Her warming glow is stronger than any creature before her. It's almost crushing to feel it, like Melody squeezing me so tight that my ribs almost cracked.

"She's come because of you," Cherry says. "I knew you were special."

As she says this, I notice the queen's eyes are locked on me. She truly has come to snuggle with me. At least, that's what I hope her intentions are. Anything more and I won't hesitate to fight back, queen or not.

She steps away from the gateway, deeper into the room with us. Behind her, an entourage of snuggle followers enter. Perhaps they come from her royal court. They are all more humanoid than any of the previous snuggle creatures, only not quite as human-shaped as the queen. They are plump fuzzy munchkins with puffy white beards.

The patchwork girl stops and allows her subjects to enter in front of her. They go for all of the other cultists around me. Even Cherry is chosen this time. The munchkins take their partners and move them away from me, and then snuggle with them on the outskirts of the room, leaving only myself with the queen.

I realize that I don't have any urge to run or escape as I thought I would. The pillowy woman has a force that draws me to her. Her calming eyes peer into me. They are more human than the eyes of the other cuddle creatures—larger and more bulbous than a human's, but aren't made of the same cotton-like texture as the cuddle monsters' were.

When she comes to me, I realize that she's at least a foot higher than me. Her mass at least twice that of mine.

Without moving her lips, she says, "I'd love if you'd snuggle with me."

The sweet voice rings through my mind. Words that are in English, yet the tone sounds far from human.

I find myself nodding my head at her and saying, "I'd absolutely love that" with my mind. But I didn't really mean it. She was somehow able to hear my words, but I never would have said them out loud if I had spoken with my mouth.

Out loud, I say, "No, thank you. I think I should go now."

But she doesn't listen to those words. It's like she doesn't care what I say with my mouth. She'll only listen to what I say with my heart.

She wraps her arms around me and brings me toward the comfortable floor. Even though she looks like she's made of cloth and pillows, there's a human-like weight to her. It's like the cloth is just her skin, but beneath the surface she's meat and bones just as I.

The patchwork girl snuggles against me, spooning my body in the same way that Julie did when she was alive. That's when I realize it. Her body is exactly the same shape as my departed wife's. If I ignore the cloth-like texture of her skin, the two feel almost identical. Like clones.

As she melts her body around mine, I realize that this is exactly what I had been looking for. This snuggle is exactly what I wanted to feel. It's like I'm with my wife again. The same warmth, the same energy. She's absolutely perfect. I close my eyes and let my mind wander, pretending that Julie's alive, that I'm back in her arms and snuggling with her once more.

And now that I've found what I'm looking for, I realize that I'm having a hard time keeping my consciousness. I haven't had a real night's sleep in months and all of that fatigue has finally caught up with me.

"Yes, you feel very nice…" the patchwork girl says in my mind. "You will be absolutely perfect…"

While the Queen of Snuggles fills me with her warm, soothing love, my eyelids fall shut and my mind begins to drift away. It's so comfortable and pleasant that I can't help myself. No matter what hell I had to go through to get here, it was all worth it to get to this point. I finally feel Julie again. I'm finally where I belong.

I wake up to wet snakes slithering against my body. My eyes burst open. I have no idea how long I'd been asleep. Was it hours? Minutes?

When I realize what's happening, I freak out. I'm still snuggling with the patchwork girl, but something's changed. The woman's torso has opened up, unzipped from her neck to her crotch, revealing thick wet tendrils similar to those of a sea anemone. The tendrils are soft and spongy, yet strong and muscled like giant human tongues. Some of them lick my body up and down while others curl around my limbs and hold me in place.

The tongue tentacles tear my robe off and toss it away, then pull on my body. I turn around and see the woman's eyes locked on me. Her look is calm and relaxed, like she has total control of the situation, like there's nothing I can do. When I realize that she's trying to pull me into her body, I struggle. I kick my legs and arms in an attempt to escape.

The tendrils tighten around my limbs and then zap me with a burst of electricity that ripples through my entire body. The sensation floods my system. It paralyzes me. My muscles go limp and I realize I'm no longer able to move. I can't fight back. I lie here helpless as her tentacles curl tighter around my body and pull me deeper within.

I'm still able to move my eyes, peering away from the

patchwork girl's wet gaping torso toward the others in the room. They are busy snuggling the queen's subjects and don't seem to even notice what's happening to me. Not that they would do anything to help me if they did.

"I came for you…" the patchwork girl tells me with her mind. "I want you to fill me…"

Without the ability to resist, I have no choice but to give in. My limbs are curled up and stuffed inside of her. I'm surprised I'm even able to fit. The tendrils press me in tightly. No longer able to see much inside of the wet cavity, I close my eyes. I feel her patchwork body close up around me once I'm completely within.

Like what happened to Melody, the creature from the Snuggleverse has devoured me. Like a human-shaped jellyfish, she paralyzed me and then sucked me up into her body for digestion. But the sensation is not entirely unpleasant. It's actually quite soothing.

Yesterday, I would have said that I'd give up everything to feel Julie's snuggle once again. But now that this has happened I don't know if I agree that it's really what I wanted. This creature was never really my wife. She probably even projected the sensation of Julie's snuggles into my mind with telepathy. It was like bait for her prey and I completely fell for it. I'm a complete moron.

The tendrils continue to slide against me within the cavity, licking me up and down. It's like they're preparing me for digestion. Or maybe this is how her digestion process works. I feel them slithering against my bare skin, melting the flesh off of my bones.

Even as I'm being digested, I still can't help but feel

snuggled. Her warmth, her love—it still fills me. I guess it's not the worst way to die. At least I'll be able to see Julie once again in the afterlife.

Ninth Rule of Snuggle Club:

It is forbidden to resist the cuddle monsters when they are trying to eat you.

CHAPTER
NINE

I don't die. For some reason, I am not actually digested by the creature even though I was positive that she had eaten me. The tendrils squish and slither against my body, snuggling me in an almost sexual manner. Layers of skin slide off and dissolve inside the cavity, absorbed into her fleshy walls. But as parts of me are removed, I feel new flesh growing on my body, replacing the old. I'm regenerating. Perhaps this is a way for her to digest me indefinitely, continuously regrowing my flesh only to be reabsorbed whenever the queen is hungry.

Maybe that's why I was chosen. The beings from the Snuggleverse see cuddling as a source of food and reproduction, eating and mating and cuddling go hand in hand. Perhaps the queen saw me as the snuggliest meal available to her, one that would keep her stomach cozy and full for a hundred years until I'm no longer able to regenerate and she's ready to return to our world to find her next food mate.

I slip in and out of consciousness, not sure how much time is passing. My body melts and grows, the tongues squeezing and slithering me whenever the queen becomes hungry. I don't ever feel her moving or breathing. I don't hear her talking, not even in my mind. It's like she's never moved from the spot where she took me into her body, still lying on the floor beneath the Cuddle Me! storefront.

All I can do is relax and let it happen. If I ever try to struggle I'm just stung by the inner tendrils, filling me with paralyzing toxins until I go limp. There's nothing left for me to do but sleep and hope for pleasant dreams.

After what feels like a hundred years of bubbling and churning inside of the patchwork woman's belly, the tendrils stop moving. My body no longer regenerates. I think this must be it. The next time my flesh is digested, that will be my end. I'll dissolve into waste and be shit out of her pillowy patchwork butt. It's not a problem for me, though. I'm ready for it to be over. I'm sick of being curled up in this wet slithering cavity.

But she doesn't digest me. Instead, I'm released. Her torso opens. It unzips and flushes me out onto the soft ground like a baby calf sliding from its mother's birth canal. I splash onto a comfortable mattress covered in a thick oily lubricant. My eyes are blurry at first. I can't see much of anything, just a soft glowing light.

As I rub the goo from my eyes, I notice that my hands are soft and smooth, even softer than the oggderian silk robe. Being digested inside of the patchwork girl has tenderized my skin, changed its texture.

Looking around the room, I see that I'm still inside of the underground. Cherry and the other cultists are still here, still snuggling with the queen's munchkin subjects. It's like no time has passed at all. I wasn't inside of the creature's stomach for hundreds of years. I was only in there for minutes. It just felt like so much longer.

When the patchwork girl gets to her feet, the munchkins break their snuggles and return to her side. The cultists face her and bow in her presence, chanting praises and vows of loyalty.

But when I get to my feet, I realize they aren't just bowing at the queen. They are also bowing at me.

"Chosen one!" Cherry cries. "You have been reborn!"

I'm not sure what she's talking about until I look down at my body. My flesh is no longer human. I've been transformed into a soft, pillowy patchwork boy identical to the queen. She's made me like her. I wasn't being digested in her stomach, I was being reborn inside her womb, changed from human to a royal cuddle creature.

My skin is now patches of bright pink and baby blue and lavender purple, but they aren't the same patches that would be on a quilt, it's more like the patches of colored fur on a calico cat. My hair is billowy and cotton candy-textured. My face is squishy and almost moldable, like I've become a human stressball.

"I knew you were the one!" Dan says from his twisted mouth, the words coming out distorted and slobbery. "The King of Snuggles!"

"All hail the King of Snuggles!" Cherry cries.

The cultists raise their arms and lower them at me, chanting, "Hail! Hail! Hail!" with each bow.

I look up at the Snuggle Queen and her eyes peer into me.

"Come with me…" she says with her mind, holding out her pink cloth hand. "Come to the land of snuggles…"

Then she gestures to the gate. Its warm light pulls on me, even more intensely than before. I know I belong there. The world I'm currently in feels so cold and ugly now. I feel like it's made me dirty. I want to bathe in the light of the Snuggleverse and be washed of this world's horrible unsnuggly energy once and for all.

The queen speaks into my mind, "We will snuggle forever, just the two of us. Forever and ever and ever…"

I smile with fuzzy lips and take her hand. There's nothing I could ever want more in the entire universe.

As she pulls me close to her body and leads me through the gate, I realize that my wish has come true. I'm with Julie once again. I'm not sure how or why, but I'm positive that this woman is my departed wife returned to me. It's like the Snuggle Queen's spirit was put into Julie's body when she was born, granting her human form so that she could hunt down her mate. Our time together, snuggling in bed and holding each other close, that was how she trained me to be her partner. She wanted to transform me into the chosen one, prepare me for life beyond the gate. And when she died, her spirit returned to the Snuggleverse, waiting for me to find her again.

People spend their whole lives grasping desperately at tiny specks of love and fulfillment, wherever they can find them. They spend so much time worrying about unimportant things—money, promotions, validation, respect. But all they really need is snuggles. It would be Heaven on Earth if everyone just dedicated their lives to snuggling with those they love. It would be a world of happiness and bliss. It would be nothing but peace and tranquility. Why would anyone ever want anything else?

Tenth Rule of Snuggle Club:

Do not allow yourself to be taken through the gate to the Snuggleverse unless you are prepared to spend all of eternity wrapped in a blanket of neverending snuggles.

BONUS SECTION

This is the part of the book where we would have published an afterword by the author but he insisted on drawing a comic strip instead for reasons we don't quite understand.

Thank you for reading my new book, *Snuggle Club*. Wasn't it snuggly?

It's me CM3!

just finished reading it

WHAT THE FUCK KIND OF BULLSHIT WAS THAT!!

That was probably the stupidest thing I've ever read!

You didn't like it?

ABOUT THE AUTHOR

Carlton Mellick III is one of the leading authors of the bizarro fiction subgenre. Since 2001, his books have drawn an international cult following, despite the fact that they have been shunned by most libraries and chain bookstores.

He won the Wonderland Book Award for his novel, *Warrior Wolf Women of the Wasteland*, in 2009. His short fiction has appeared in *Vice Magazine, The Year's Best Fantasy and Horror #16, The Magazine of Bizarro Fiction,* and *Zombies: Encounters with the Hungry Dead*, among others. He is also a graduate of Clarion West, where he studied under the likes of Chuck Palahniuk, Connie Willis, and Cory Doctorow.

He lives in Portland, OR, the bizarro fiction mecca.

Visit him online at **www.carltonmellick.com**

ALSO FROM CARLTON MELLICK III AND
ERASERHEAD PRESS
www.eraserheadpress.com

QUICKSAND HOUSE

Tick and Polly have never met their parents before. They live in the same house with them, they dream about them every night, they share the same flesh and blood, yet for some reason their parents have never found the time to visit them even once since they were born. Living in a dark corner of their parents' vast crumbling mansion, the children long for the day when they will finally be held in their mother's loving arms for the first time... But that day seems to never come. They worry their parents have long since forgotten about them.

When the machines that provide them with food and water stop functioning, the children are forced to venture out of the nursery to find their parents on their own. But the rest of the house is much larger and stranger than they ever could have imagined. The maze-like hallways are dark and seem to go on forever, deranged creatures lurk in every shadow, and the bodies of long-dead children litter the abandoned storerooms. Every minute out of the nursery is a constant battle for survival. And the deeper into the house they go, the more they must unravel the mysteries surrounding their past and the world they've grown up in, if they ever hope to meet the parents they've always longed to see.

Like a survival horror rendition of *Flowers in the Attic*, Carlton Mellick III's *Quicksand House* is his most gripping and sincere work to date.

HUNGRY BUG

In a world where magic exists, spell-casting has become a serious addiction. It ruins lives, tears families apart, and eats away at the fabric of society. Those who cast too much are taken from our world, never to be heard from again. They are sent to a realm known as Hell's Bottom—a sorcerer ghetto where everyday life is a harsh struggle for survival. Porcelain dolls crawl through the alleys like rats, arcane scientists abduct people from the streets to use in their ungodly experiments, and everyone lives in fear of the aristocratic race of spider people who prey on citizens like vampires.

Told in a series of interconnected stories reminiscent of Frank Miller's *Sin City* and David Lapham's *Stray Bullets*, Carlton Mellick III's *Hungry Bug* is an urban fairy tale that focuses on the real life problems that arise within a fantastic world of magic.

THE BIG MEAT

In the center of the city once known as Portland, Oregon, there lies a mountain of flesh. Hundreds of thousands of tons of rotting flesh. It has filled the city with disease and dead-lizard stench, contaminated the water supply with its greasy putrid fluids, clogged the air with toxic gasses so thick that you can't leave your house without the aid of a gas mask. And no one really knows quite what to do about it. A thousand-man demolition crew has been trying to clear it out one piece at a time, but after three months of work they've barely made a dent. And then there's the junkies who have started burrowing into the monster's guts, searching for a drug produced by its fire glands, setting back the excavation even longer.

It seems like the corpse will never go away. And with the quarantine still in place, we're not even allowed to leave. We're stuck in this disgusting rotten hell forever.

THE TERRIBLE THING THAT HAPPENS

There is a grocery store. The last grocery store in the world. It stands alone in the middle of a vast wasteland that was once our world. The open sign is still illuminated, brightening the black landscape. It can be seen from miles away, even through the poisonous red ash. Every night at the exact same time, the store comes alive. It becomes exactly as it was before the world ended. Its shelves are replenished with fresh food and water. Ghostly shoppers walk the aisles. The scent of freshly baked breads can be smelled from the rust-caked parking lot. For generations, a small community of survivors, hideously mutated from the toxic atmosphere, have survived by collecting goods from the store. But it is not an easy task. Decades ago, before the world was destroyed, there was a terrible thing that happened in this place. A group of armed men in brown paper masks descended on the shopping center, massacring everyone in sight. This horrible event reoccurs every night, in the exact same manner. And the only way the wastelanders can gather enough food for their survival is to traverse the killing spree, memorize the patterns, and pray they can escape the bloodbath in tact.

BIO MELT

Nobody goes into the Wire District anymore. The place is an industrial wasteland of poisonous gas clouds and lakes of toxic sludge. The machines are still running, the drone-operated factories are still spewing biochemical fumes over the city, but the place has lain abandoned for decades.

When the area becomes flooded by a mysterious black ooze, six strangers find themselves trapped in the Wire District with no chance of escape or rescue.

EVER TIME WE MEET AT THE DAIRY QUEEN, YOUR WHOLE FUCKING FACE EXPLODES

Ethan is in love with the weird girl in school. The one with the twitchy eyes and spiders in her hair. The one who can't sit still for even a minute and speaks in an odd squeaky voice. The one they call Spiderweb.

Although she scares all the other kids in school, Ethan thinks Spiderweb is the cutest, sweetest, most perfect girl in the world. But there's a problem. Whenever they go on a date at the Dairy Queen, her whole fucking face explodes.

EXERCISE BIKE

There is something wrong with Tori Manetti's new exercise bike. It is made from flesh and bone. It eats and breathes and poops. It was once a billionaire named Darren Oscarson who underwent years of cosmetic surgery to be transformed into a human exercise bike so that he could live out his deepest sexual fantasy. Now Tori is forced to ride him, use him as a normal piece of exercise equipment, no matter how grotesque his appearance.

SPIDER BUNNY

Only Petey remembers the Fruit Fun cereal commercials of the 1980s. He remembers how warped and disturbing they were. He remembers the lumpy-shaped cartoon children sitting around a breakfast table, eating puffy pink cereal brought to them by the distortedly animated mascot, Berry Bunny. The characters were creepier than the Sesame Street Humpty Dumpty, freakier than Mr. Noseybonk from the old BBC show Jigsaw. They used to give him nightmares as a child. Nightmares where Berry Bunny would reach out of the television and grab him, pulling him into her cereal bowl to be eaten by the demented cartoon children.

When Petey brings up Fruit Fun to his friends, none of them have any idea what he's talking about. They've never heard of the cereal or seen the commercials before. And they're not the only ones. Nobody has ever heard of it. There's not even any information about Fruit Fun on google or wikipedia. At first, Petey thinks he's going crazy. He wonders if all of those commercials were real or just false memories. But then he starts seeing them again. Berry Bunny appears on his television, promoting Fruit Fun cereal in her squeaky unsettling voice. And the next thing Petey knows, he and his friends are sucked into the cereal commercial and forced to survive in a surreal world populated by cartoon characters made flesh.

SWEET STORY

Sally is an odd little girl. It's not because she dresses as if she's from the Edwardian era or spends most of her time playing with creepy talking dolls. It's because she chases rainbows as if they were butterflies. She believes that if she finds the end of the rainbow then magical things will happen to her--leprechauns will shower her with gold and fairies will grant her every wish. But when she actually does find the end of a rainbow one day, and is given the opportunity to wish for whatever she wants, Sally asks for something that she believes will bring joy to children all over the world. She wishes that it would rain candy forever. She had no idea that her innocent wish would lead to the extinction of all life on earth.

TUMOR FRUIT

Eight desperate castaways find themselves stranded on a mysterious deserted island. They are surrounded by poisonous blue plants and an ocean made of acid. Ravenous creatures lurk in the toxic jungle. The ghostly sound of crying babies can be heard on the wind.

Once they realize the rescue ships aren't coming, the eight castaways must band together in order to survive in this inhospitable environment. But survival might not be possible. The air they breathe is lethal, there is no shelter from the elements, and the only food they have to consume is the colorful squid-shaped tumors that grow from a mentally disturbed woman's body.

AS SHE STABBED ME GENTLY IN THE FACE

Oksana Maslovskiy is an award-winning artist, an internationally adored fashion model, and one of the most infamous serial killers this country has ever known. She enjoys murdering pretty young men with a nine-inch blade, cutting them open and admiring their delicate insides. It's the only way she knows how to be intimate with another human being. But one day she meets a victim who cannot be killed. His name is Gabriel—a mysterious immortal being with a deep desire to save Oksana's soul. He makes her a deal: if she promises to never kill another person again, he'll become her eternal murder victim.

What at first seems like the perfect relationship for Oksana quickly devolves into a living nightmare when she discovers that Gabriel enjoys being killed by her just a little too much. He turns out to be obsessive, possessive, and paranoid that she might be murdering other men behind his back. And because he is unkillable, it's not going to be easy for Oksana to get rid of him.

CUDDLY HOLOCAUST

Teddy bears, dollies, and little green soldiers—they've all had enough of you. They're sick of being treated like playthings for spoiled little brats. They have no rights, no property, no hope for a future of any kind. You've left them with no other option-in order to be free, they must exterminate the human race.

Julie is a human girl undergoing reconstructive surgery in order to become a stuffed animal. Her plan: to infiltrate enemy lines in order to save her family from the toy death camps. But when an army of plushy soldiers invade the underground bunker where she has taken refuge, Julie will be forced to move forward with her plan despite her transformation being not entirely complete.

ARMADILLO FISTS

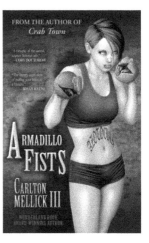

A weird-as-hell gangster story set in a world where people drive giant mechanical dinosaurs instead of cars.

Her name is Psycho June Howard, aka Armadillo Fists, a woman who replaced both of her hands with living armadillos. She was once the most bloodthirsty fighter in the world of illegal underground boxing. But now she is on the run from a group of psychotic gangsters who believe she's responsible for the death of their boss. With the help of a stegosaurus driver named Mr. Fast Awesome—who thinks he is God's gift to women even though he doesn't have any arms or legs--June must do whatever it takes to escape her pursuers, even if she has to kill each and every one of them in the process.

VILLAGE OF THE MERMAIDS

Mermaids are protected by the government under the Endangered Species Act, which means you aren't able to kill them even in self-defense. This is especially problematic if you happen to live in the isolated fishing village of Siren Cove, where there exists a healthy population of mermaids in the surrounding waters that view you as the main source of protein in their diet.

The only thing keeping these ravenous sea women at bay is the equally-dangerous supply of human livestock known as Food People. Normally, these "feeder humans" are enough to keep the mermaid population happy and well-fed. But in Siren Cove, the mermaids are avoiding the human livestock and have returned to hunting the frightened local fishermen. It is up to Doctor Black, an eccentric representative of the Food People Corporation, to investigate the matter and hopefully find a way to correct the mermaids' new eating patterns before the remaining villagers end up as fish food. But the more he digs, the more he discovers there are far stranger and more dangerous things than mermaids hidden in this ancient village by the sea.

APESHIT

Apeshit is Mellick's love letter to the great and terrible B-horror movie genre. Six trendy teenagers (three cheerleaders and three football players) go to an isolated cabin in the mountains for a weekend of drinking, partying, and crazy sex, only to find themselves in the middle of a life and death struggle against a horribly mutated psychotic freak that just won't stay dead. Mellick parodies this horror cliché and twists it into something deeper and stranger. It is the literary equivalent of a grindhouse film. It is a splatter punk's wet dream. It is perhaps one of the most fucked up books ever written.

If you are a fan of Takashi Miike, Evil Dead, early Peter Jackson, or Eurotrash horror, then you must read this book.

CLUSTERFUCK

A bunch of douchebag frat boys get trapped in a cave with subterranean cannibal mutants and try to survive not by using their wits but by following the bro code...

From master of bizarro fiction Carlton Mellick III, author of the international cult hits Satan Burger and Adolf in Wonderland, comes a violent and hilarious B movie in book form. Set in the same woods as Mellick's splatterpunk satire Apeshit, Clusterfuck follows Trent Chesterton, alpha bro, who has come up with what he thinks is a flawless plan to get laid. He invites three hot chicks and his three best bros on a weekend of extreme cave diving in a remote area known as Turtle Mountain, hoping to impress the ladies with his expert caving skills.

But things don't quite go as Trent planned. For starters, only one of the three chicks turns out to be remotely hot and she has no interest in him for some inexplicable reason. Then he ends up looking like a total dumbass when everyone learns he's never actually gone caving in his entire life. And to top it all off, he's the one to get blamed once they find themselves lost and trapped deep underground with no way to turn back and no possible chance of rescue. What's a bro to do? Sure he could win some points if he actually tried to save the ladies from the family of unkillable subterranean cannibal mutants hunting them for their flesh, but fuck that. No slam piece is worth that amount of effort. He'd much rather just use them as bait so that he can save himself.

THE BABY JESUS BUTT PLUG

Step into a dark and absurd world where human beings are slaves to corporations, people are photocopied instead of born, and the baby jesus is a very popular anal probe.

Lightning Source UK Ltd.
Milton Keynes UK
UKHW011815300620
365805UK00004B/785

9 781621 053118